"Don't worry. I'm not going to kiss you again."

She resisted the urge to swallow. "What makes you think I'm worried?"

The cynical slant of his lips belied the faint gleam of amusement in his eyes. "Probably the way you're sidling up to me like I'm a hungry coyote."

"Nothing wrong with a coyote," she quipped. "At least he mates for life."

His nostrils flared. "Like I said before, I don't plan on kissing you again."

For some reason, his cocky promise raked over every womanly particle inside of Dallas and before she realized what she was doing, she'd moved close enough to stick her face right in front of his. "I think you're the one who's worried, Boone."

She watched his gaze drop to her lips, and anticipation shivered right through her.

"Me?" he asked softly. "What do I have to be worried about?"

"That you kissed me—and you liked it."

Dear Reader,

Christmas is coming! The mere words make me want to dig out the decorations, bake all sorts of gooey, decadent desserts and race to the mall to shop, shop, shop! But mostly, Christmas turns my thoughts to family, the warm gatherings we've had through the years and the love we've always given to one another.

My heroine, Dallas Donovan, has never been away from her family during the holidays and when she unexpectedly finds herself a thousand miles from home, she can't bear to miss all the fun of gift giving and celebrations. But she also understands that Christmas is more than parties, it's a time of hope and dreams and sharing.

On the other hand, my hero, Boone Barnett, has forgotten how to celebrate anything. For the past years, he and his young daughter have gone through one lonely Christmas after another and Dallas soon sees that the two of them need her to fill their lives with cheer and love.

I want to personally thank all of you for continuing to read my Men of the West stories and I hope you enjoy this trip that Dallas takes to rugged Nevada, where she teaches a rancher all about sharing his heart.

Merry Christmas and God bless you all!

Stella Bagwell

CHRISTMAS WITH THE MUSTANG MAN

STELLA BAGWELL

Harlequin®

SPECIAL EDITION

Recycling programs
for this product may
not exist in your area.

ISBN-13: 978-0-373-65641-7

CHRISTMAS WITH THE MUSTANG MAN

Other titles by Stella Bagwell available in ebook

STELLA BAGWELL

has written more than seventy novels for Harlequin and Silhouette Books. She credits her loyal readers and hopes her stories have brightened their lives in some small way.

A cowgirl through and through, she loves to watch old Westerns, and has recently learned how to rope a steer. Her days begin and end helping her husband care for a beloved herd of horses on their little ranch located on the south Texas coast. When she's not ropin' and ridin', you'll find her at her desk, creating her next tale of love.

The couple have a son, who is a high school math teacher and athletic coach. Stella loves to hear from readers and invites them to contact her at stellabagwell@gmail.com.

To my late mother, Lucille, who always
made Christmas a special time for her family.

When gifts were spare, her love was rich.

Chapter One

"What the hell?"

Boone Barnett's muttered question was lost in the cold wind as he watched a truck pulling a horse van leave a wake of dust as it barreled its way across the desert basin. The woman from New Mexico, he decided. The rig was too fancy to belong to anyone around here. But she was supposed to have been here shortly after lunch. Not five minutes from sundown!

Damn it, he was chilled to the bone, exhausted and hungry. He was hardly in the mood to put up with a woman who'd not had the forethought or good manners to show up at a decent hour. If she expected to look at the horses now, she was in for a surprise, Boone thought. His horses weren't pampered pets housed in luxurious stalls with overhead lights. They existed outside, as they had for hundreds of years on this Nevada range.

Dropping the feed sack near the barn door, he called

to a barking black-and-white shepherd before starting the long walk to the front of the house. Frigid north wind had been gusting all day and since he'd been outdoors for most of it, his face burned from exposure and his feet weren't in much better shape. While he waited for the truck to pull to a stop, he stomped his boots and prayed for a little feeling to return to his toes.

Next to his leg, the dog whined and Boone's gloved hand patted the animal's head. "You don't need to worry about the lady, Queenie. She's only a visitor."

Pricking its ears, the shepherd followed Boone forward, while a few feet away, the driver's door opened on the truck and a tall, shapely woman stepped to the ground. She was dressed in blue jeans and boots and a bright red sweater, and as she moved toward him, she quickly shoved her arms into a denim ranch jacket.

"Hello," she called out loud enough to be heard above the wind.

"Hello," he greeted in response.

As the two of them met on the bare, hard-packed earth, Boone removed his glove and extended his hand to her. Even though he was damned irritated at her for showing up at a ridiculous hour, she was still a potential client. And for the past few months horse buyers hadn't exactly been beating down his door. The last thing he wanted to do was offend this one with bad manners.

"I'm Boone Barnett," he introduced himself. "And you must be Ms. Donovan?"

A wide smile spread her cherry-colored lips and Boone found himself staring at the woman. He'd not been to town in weeks and even when he was there he didn't take much notice of people, especially women, but something about the warmth on her face had struck him.

She was far younger than he'd expected and definitely

prettier. Light, copper-red hair fell in thick waves to her shoulders and with each gust of wind, it tossed around her head like a bright silk scarf.

She grasped his hand in a firm shake while dimples bracketed her lips and Boone suddenly realized it was going to be an effort to do business with this woman. She had an irritating ability to remind him he was a man, one that had lived without a woman for a long, long time.

"That's right," she said. "Call me Dallas. And I want to apologize for showing up so late this evening. The trip out here took much longer than I expected. My truck kept trying to quit on me."

He'd expected to hear some sort of excuse for her tardiness, but not this one. "It appeared to be running just fine when you pulled up a few moments ago," he couldn't stop himself from pointing out.

A faint line furrowed the center of her pale forehead. "For the past mile or two it seemed to smooth out. But several times during the trip out here the engine choked down to a crawl and died. I filled the tank with fuel at Pioche and I'm beginning to wonder if water might have been in the diesel."

He studied the tiny movements of expression crossing her face and decided her explanation was sincere. Not that the reason for her tardiness mattered, but her honesty did. He wasn't about to let even one of his horses go to someone who lied. Liars tended to have other faults and his mustangs were like his children. Once they left for a new home, he wanted them to be in the best of hands.

"Could be you picked up some bad fuel," he agreed. "But whatever the problem, let's hope it's fixed itself."

She let out a long breath. "I hope so, too. The truck belongs to my brother. He was kind enough to let me bring it on this trip, but he won't be very happy with me if the engine is ruined. Especially since the truck is practically new."

The realization that he was still holding her hand suddenly hit Boone and though his first instinct was to drop it like a hot brick, he released it slowly and then jammed his hand deep into the pocket of his coat.

She pulled a thick white scarf from the pocket on her jacket and as she quickly wrapped it around her neck, she said, "I tried calling, to give you a heads-up that I was going to be late. But my cell couldn't pick up a signal."

He tried to smile, but his face was stiff from the cold. Not that he could use the brutal weather as an excuse. These past few years Boone had pretty much forgotten how to lift the corners of his mouth. But something about this woman made him want to try to appear friendly and normal, even if he wasn't particularly feeling that way.

"Cell phones are useless out here," he informed her. "We're too far away from civilization to have a signal tower anywhere near."

The wind continued to blow her hair in all directions, and she caught the wayward strands with one hand as she turned her head and surveyed the open land around them. Although her clothes were casual, she wore them with class and it was easy for Boone to see that she'd not purchased them from a discount store. No, this lady was first-class all the way.

"I thought our ranch was isolated, but this place has the Diamond D beat all to pieces," she remarked. "I don't think I passed another house for the past fifteen miles."

Because she'd contacted him by phone before she'd made the trip, Boone was already aware that this young woman lived in southern New Mexico, ran a riding stable for handicapped children and was interested in purchasing mustangs. Other than those bits of information, he knew nothing about her personally. But he was definitely learning fast.

He asked, "Is there someone else still sitting in the truck? You didn't travel all this way alone, did you?"

She smiled again and his gaze automatically focused on the twinkle in her eyes. Was she just the happy sort, he wondered, or was this her way of flirting?

A woman like her flirting with a man like you? Hell, Boone, you're really losing it.

"I made the trip by myself. None of my family or friends was available to travel with me this time."

Boone's gaze zeroed in on her ring finger. Did her family include a husband? He couldn't imagine this young, attractive woman was still single. But there was no ring of any sort on her left hand.

Why are you wondering about any of that, Boone? Dallas Donovan is here to buy horses. Her marital status is none of your business.

Stunned that he'd let his curiosity wander so far, Boone did his best to jerk his focus back on the real purpose of this woman's visit.

"Well, I'm glad you made the trip safely, only there's not much daylight left." He gestured toward a maze of outbuildings and connecting corrals. "You're welcome to look around while I finish spreading feed. There's a yard lamp on the left side of the big barn. You might be able to see a few of the horses I've corralled there."

"Sure," she happily agreed. "Now that I'm here, I'd love to see what I can."

The man turned away from her and started walking toward a long, low barn with several adjoining corrals. Dallas fell in step beside him and as they moved along, she purposely fastened her gaze upon their destination.

Yet keeping her eyes off Boone Barnett did little to push him out of her thoughts.

Meeting this man in person had been like a wham on the head. Something about him had instantly grabbed her attention and still hadn't let go. Maybe because the real thing was a far cry from the image she'd formed when she'd spoken to him over the phone.

First of all, she'd been expecting him to be at least in his fifties or sixties. Instead, he appeared to be just a few years older than her thirty-two. And secondly, he was very tall. At five foot nine, it wasn't often that Dallas encountered a man that was a head taller than her, but Boone Barnett was that and more. And from the width of his shoulders beneath the plaid jacket, his height was backed up by a very solid foundation.

Even in the waning light, she could see his features were lean and hawkish and tanned to a nut-brown color. The somberness of his face both intrigued and bothered Dallas. She hated to think he might be a man plagued with worries and troubles. It was hard to do business with a person who couldn't see the lighter side of things.

At the front of the largest barn, he picked up a red plastic feed bucket and pointed to a corral to their immediate left. "There's a small herd of yearlings in that pen. The mares are next to them. Look all you want, I'll be back in a few minutes."

Glancing at him, she offered politely, "Is there anything I can do to help?"

He shook his head. "Thanks, but I can manage."

Before she could make any sort of reply, he walked away and she was left to make her way over to the penned horses. Apparently he'd already spread the feed for this small herd. The animals were presently lined up to long wooden troughs filled with mixed grains. Nearby, a hay manger was stuffed full of dark green alfalfa.

From what she could see, the horses were well-groomed and in great shape, but as far as Dallas was concerned, their dispositions and willingness to please were more important traits. For the sake of the children, she had to make sure the mounts that made up Angel Wings Stables were dependable, trustworthy steeds.

She was still standing at the fence and sizing up the mares, when Boone finally reappeared. Darkness had now settled over the ranch yard and across the way, near the barn porch, a yard light flickered on to shed a weak glow across the dusty pens.

When he finally came to a stop a few feet away from her, she waited for him to speak.

"The geldings and stallions are penned on the back side of the barn," he said to her. "But it's very dark over there. It would be better if you looked at them tomorrow."

"You don't have to persuade me," she said with agreement. "It's getting colder out here."

"I'm finished with all the outside chores. Let's go to the house where it's warm," he suggested.

Dallas looked at him, but there wasn't much to glean from his stoic features. It was impossible for her to tell if he actually welcomed her arrival on the ranch or was simply tolerating it. She probably should have stayed in Pioche and waited until morning to drive out here, she thought dismally. But once she'd checked in at a hotel and grabbed a bite to eat, she'd believed there was plenty of time to make the last leg of her journey to White River Ranch.

She'd never dreamed the drive out here would be so long and the terrain so rough. And she especially hadn't expected Liam's truck to start giving her problems. Now she was going to have to make a second trip out here, which would ultimately cause her to be a day late in getting back home to the Diamond D. And that thought was already weighing on her shoulders.

"I don't want to intrude on you and your family, Mr. Barnett," she said as she quickened her pace to match his longer strides.

"My name is Boone," he insisted. "And since it's just me and my daughter, you won't be intruding."

He had a deep, rough voice that was far more expressive than his face. Each time he spoke, his words seemed to vibrate right through her.

"Thank you, Boone. It would be nice to warm up for a minute or two," she said, while wondering if his remark meant that he wasn't married or that Mrs. Barnett was simply not home this evening. Either way, it was none of her business. The man was extending her a bit of hospitality and she needed to accept it graciously, the way her parents had taught her.

At a small, screened-in back porch, he held the door open for her, then did the same with a wooden door that entered the house. Trying not to put too much thought in his huge presence looming just behind her, Dallas stepped inside and found herself in a small kitchen that smelled of baking pizza.

"Have a seat at the table," he invited. "I'll get us something to drink. You like coffee?"

"Love it. But don't go to any trouble," she told him as she made her way across the room to a small round table. Piled atop it was a child's backpack with several textbooks spilling from its open lid. Next to the books was a soda can and lying next to that, on a paper towel, a half-eaten sandwich.

Dallas pulled off her coat and placed the garment on

the back of a chair, then turned to see the Nevada rancher had already removed his coat and hung it on a peg by the door. The sight of him in the stark kitchen light, without the bulky jacket hiding his frame, jolted her. He was as solid as a rock and everything about him shouted the word *man*.

"I'd be making a pot whether you were here or not," he explained. On his way to the cabinets, he caught sight of the cluttered table and instantly changed course. "Here, let me clear that away. Hayley's not very good about putting her things in her room."

Dallas chuckled. "I never was a tidy child. My mother was constantly nagging me and my younger sister to put our things where they belonged. Our older sister never got nagged at, though. She was a neat freak."

Walking over to the table, he leaned across the expanse of worn wood to pick up the scattered items and his upper torso drew within inches of her arm. The subtle scents of hay, horses and sage drifted to Dallas's nostrils before she instinctively stepped aside to put more breathing space between them.

"So you have sisters," he stated.

Moistening her lips, she tried to calm the nervous bumping of her heart. "Two. And three brothers," she answered. "I'm in the middle of the bunch."

After placing the books and backpack on a nearby rolltop desk, he returned to fetch the sandwich and soda can.

"Well, Hayley doesn't have a mother to nag her, so I have that thankless job. And from the looks of it, I'm not getting through," he added with a grimace.

Dallas didn't make any sort of immediate reply. Since she'd never been a mother, she was hardly in a position to offer parenting advice. And without knowing exactly why his daughter's mother was absent, she might slip and inadvertently say something he'd find offensive.

Instead, she took a seat at the table and decided to slant the conversation in a different direction. "Do you have siblings, Boone?"

Across the room, he began to put the coffee fixings together. "No. It's just me. My dad lives in town, and that's it."

The information only made Dallas wonder more. Why didn't Boone's father live here on the ranch? Did the man's health require him to live closer to a doctor? she silently mused. Or maybe the elder Barnett just didn't want to live out in the remote countryside. After all, not all families lived together in one big house, like the Donovans.

"So your father isn't a rancher?"

Damn it, she was here to buy horses from the man, not make a documentary about his life, she silently scolded herself. But she couldn't seem to prevent the personal questions from popping from her mouth.

"My grandfather was a rancher. Dad never liked the work much," he answered bluntly.

Deciding it would be safer to talk about her own family, she said, "The Donovans have always raised horses—Thoroughbred racers. Lately my brothers have been tossing around the idea of putting a few cattle on the ranch or maybe a running line of quarter horses, but those are just ideas. Dad is retired...or should I say semi-retired," she added with a fond chuckle. "So he mainly lets the guys run things the way they want to."

"Sounds like the place is a family-run operation," he commented.

By now he'd shut the lid on the coffeemaker and the pungent smell of the brewing grounds was beginning to overpower the pizza. After driving hours and hours since early this morning, Dallas was definitely in need of the hot brew to fight off the weariness threatening to overtake her.

"It is. My grandparents built the Diamond D back in 1968 and most of the family still lives there together. Except for Grandfather Arthur, who passed away some years back." She paused and then added, "I noticed on the road map that this ranch is located in Lincoln County. That's the name of the county where I live."

"So you're from the part of New Mexico where the famous range wars occurred," he said thoughtfully. "And outlaws like Billy the Kid roamed the land."

Impressed by his historical knowledge, she glanced at him. "That's right. What's this Lincoln County known for?"

He shrugged. "Years ago it was all about gold and silver strikes, brothels and lawlessness. Now the mines are dead. But the ranchers have hung on."

"And the mustangs," she added.

"Yeah. Thank God for the mustangs."

The big cowboy was looking straight at her now and Dallas was finding it extremely hard to tell whether he'd spoken with sarcasm or sincerity. He had very dark eyes that had such a piercing quality she could practically feel them sliding over her face and that in itself was enough to distract her. Not to mention the fact that he'd removed his black Stetson and his streaked brown hair had slid to a boyish bang across his forehead.

He said, "It must get interesting at your house—everybody living together. Are you one big happy family or does that only happen in fairy tales or sitcoms?"

Was he saying he didn't believe families could live and love together? The cynical idea saddened her and put a hint of defensive pride in her voice as she replied, "I can truthfully say that ninety percent of the time we're all pretty happy."

"That must be nice," he said lowly.

"It is nice," she agreed. "Being with my family is everything to me."

He turned his back to her and reached up to retrieve two cups from a cabinet shelf. At the table, a pent-up breath whooshed out of Dallas. What was the matter with her? Living on a horse ranch, she'd dealt with all sorts of men before. This one wasn't necessarily any different. Except that Boone Barnett looked a little sexier, a whole lot tougher and a bit more seasoned than most.

So what if he was all those things? Dallas mentally argued with herself. After being dumped only days before her wedding, she'd learned to view men and their charms with skeptical indifference, especially men that she didn't know. She couldn't allow this hunk of male muscle to recklessly turn her head.

Across the room, Boone filled two mugs with coffee while thoughtfully mulling over Dallas Donovan's remark. Maybe this woman and her "nice" family were for real. But he had a hard time buying into the idea. The Barnetts had always been fractured in some unfortunate way and he'd never been around an extended family that interacted with love and respect for each other.

Yet, in spite of that, he couldn't say that his family life had always been lacking. For a while, when Boone had been a young boy and his grandparents still living, things had been basically good for him.

Wayne and Alice Barnett had been decent, hardworking people. They'd cared about him, looked after him, given him the love and support he'd needed, while his own parents had only made a halfhearted gesture at raising their only son.

Shoving the dismal thoughts aside, he carried the mugs over to the table, along with a bowl of sugar and a carton of half-and-half. After he'd fetched a spoon and napkin for her, he took a seat across from his guest.

Now that he could see the woman in the light of the kitchen, he decided she looked even prettier than she had in the falling dusk. She had a wide soft mouth the color of a pink seashell and her pale green eyes were veiled by thick, long lashes. A rosy tinge marked her cheeks and straight little nose, and added to the vibrancy of her face. Yet it was her smile and the cheeriness in her eyes that grabbed him the most. She seemed to radiate happiness and that intrigued him, surprised him. Were there actually people like her left in the world? he wondered. Or was she simply putting up a polite front?

"So, when did you decide to add mustangs to your herd?" he asked, while watching her stir a dollop of cream into the steaming coffee. She had long fingers with plain, short nails. There were no rings on her fingers, but there was a wide-cuffed band of silver set with a red coral stone circling her right wrist. That one piece of jewelry would probably buy two months of groceries for him and his daughter.

Thoroughbreds, a six-figure truck and horse van and a family-owned ranch. Those things, coupled with her appearance, made it clear this woman was hardly lacking in financial funds.

"Several months ago a friend purchased a stallion and I was impressed at his intelligence and manners. Seeing him prompted me to look into what the mustangs were all about. That's when I discovered how many of them need homes. Have you been working with them very long?"

She seemed genuinely interested and Boone was beginning to see she wasn't simply a rich woman playing at a hobby.

"Eight years. Before that I only had cattle and a few quarter horses on the ranch. When I got my first mustang I never planned on that one animal eventually turning into a business or a love affair for me." He shrugged, while trying not to feel embarrassed for allowing this woman to see a softer part of him. "It was just something that happened."

"I—"

She suddenly broke off and lifted her gaze beyond his shoulder. Boone turned his head just in time to see his twelve-year-old-daughter, Hayley, bound into the room. As soon as the girl spotted Dallas, she skidded to a halt and stared openmouthed at their visitor.

"Oh. I didn't know you had company, Dad." Keeping her eye on the two adults, she moved past a row of cabinets until she reached a gas range. "I'm cooking pizza— for our dinner. And I think it's done."

"Hurry up with that and come over here," Boone told her. "I want you to meet our guest."

From her seat at the table, Dallas studied the young girl. Like her father, she was tall and if not a teenager already, then very close to it. Her light brown hair was bobbed short and tucked behind her ears, while her clothing was a typical T-shirt and hip-riding jeans. She wasn't a dazzling beauty by any stretch of the imagination, but she was pretty. Or at least she would be if she'd smile, Dallas decided. Apparently she took that lack of expression from her father, too.

At the stove, the girl deftly donned a pair of quilted mittens and lifted the pizza from the oven. After she placed the baked concoction on the stove top and switched the control knob to the off position, she walked over to the table and stood stiffly at her father's shoulder.

"Dallas, this is my daughter, Hayley. And, Hayley, this is Dallas Donovan. She's driven all the way from New Mexico to purchase a few of our horses."

Dallas rose to her feet and offered her hand to the girl. Hayley seemed a bit surprised to be greeted in such an adult manner, but after a slight hesitation, she placed her small hand in Dallas's.

"It's very nice to meet you, Hayley," Dallas said. "Do you help your father with the horses?"

The glance she slanted at her father said she wasn't sure how to answer that question. "Sometimes."

"With school going on I suppose you don't have much spare time," Dallas remarked.

"Not much," the girl replied. "I'm in seventh grade now and the math is awful."

Dallas chuckled. "I never did like math. My dad grounded me once because I made a D. After that I had to study or sit home for the whole school year."

Hayley's expression perked up as she seemingly decided that Dallas was human after all. "Do you have any kids, Ms. Donovan?"

"Please, call me Dallas," she said with a smile for the girl. "And no. I'm sorry to say I don't have any children."

"Then you're not married?"

"Hayley! Quit asking personal questions! It's not polite and you know better," Boone admonished.

Shaking her head, Dallas sank back into her seat at the table. "It's all right. Your daughter is curious. There's nothing wrong with that," she told Boone, then looked directly at Hayley. "No. I'm not married. What about you? Do you have a boyfriend?"

Hayley giggled and Boone shot the child a strange

look, which made Dallas wonder if the sound of his daughter laughing was a rare thing, or was it the idea of Hayley having a boyfriend that caught his attention? Either way, Dallas felt totally drawn to the girl.

"Noooo," Hayley exclaimed, her cheeks a bright pink. "I'm only twelve! Well—I'll be thirteen in four months. But Dad says that's too young for a boyfriend."

Glancing over at him, Dallas noticed that Boone Barnett's expression had returned to resembling a piece of hard granite, which only proved that he didn't quite understand a young girl's dreams and feelings.

Ignoring him for the moment, Dallas said, "Oh. Well, I just thought there might be a boy at school that you liked. You know, like best friends."

The girl's gaze instantly dropped to the floor. "The middle school I go to only has about ninety students altogether. So there aren't that many boys to pick from. But there is one that I like," she mumbled, then looked directly up at Dallas. "His name is Jeffery. And the rest of the girls call him a nerd. But I like him 'cause he's polite and smart, not dumb jerks like most of the other boys."

Dallas tossed her a smile of approval. "He sounds like a winner to me."

Hayley looked up, her eyes widened with surprise. "Really?"

"Sure. Manners and brains. That's the combination I'd pick."

Hayley cast her father a subtle look of triumph, but he said nothing on the subject. Instead, he told his daughter, "You'd better cut the pizza before it gets cold."

The girl appeared as though she wanted to say more, but at the last moment decided not to press her luck.

As Dallas watched Hayley return to the gas range to

deal with the pizza, Boone asked, "Would you like to join us, Dallas? There's plenty."

Surprised by the offer, Dallas turned her head to see he was looking at her with those dark brown eyes, surveying her in a way that left her feeling like a turtle without a shell.

"No, thanks. I'd like to get to my hotel room before it gets late."

After quickly draining the last of her coffee, she rose to her feet. Boone was out of his seat almost at the same time and reached for her heavy jacket. Dallas's heart beat fast as he held the garment for her to slip her arms into.

She was accustomed to men doing gentlemanly things for her. But she wasn't expecting such caring manners from this one. Nor was she expecting to feel so breathless, so completely aware of his strong presence.

"I'll walk you to your truck," he said. He shouldered on his own jacket and reached for a flashlight that sat on the end of a cabinet counter.

"Goodbye, Hayley," Dallas said to Boone's daughter. "It was nice meeting you."

The girl nodded shyly, then gave her a little wave before Boone opened the door and ushered Dallas out of the kitchen.

Outside, darkness had settled over the ranch and she appreciated the glow of Boone's flashlight illuminating their path as the two of them moved across the barren yard.

"Is there a special time I need to be here tomorrow?" she asked as they walked briskly toward the truck. "If you have other appointments, I can match my schedule to yours. That's the least I can do for arriving late today."

"I don't have anything pressing going on tomorrow," he replied. "Come out whenever you'd like."

As they moved along in the darkness, she realized he was close enough for her to reach over and touch, if she was so minded to. The idea titillated her senses and sent all sorts of questions hurtling through her mind. Mainly, where was Hayley's mother? And was there some other woman in this man's life?

Don't be letting your thoughts stray in that direction, Dallas. The hurt that Allen laid on your heart would be a minor scratch compared to what this cowboy could do to you. Get your business done with the man and get the heck out of here.

"I'll be out early," she promised him as she jerked her thoughts back to the real issue.

Once they reached the truck, he closed a hand around her elbow and helped her into the tall cab. Determined not to linger any longer, she closed the door between them and reached to start the engine. To her dismay the truck gave one loud sputter, and then the starter whirled uselessly.

Boone knocked on the door panel to garner her attention and then made a motion for her to lower the window. Dallas did as he asked, then hung her head over the partially opened glass panel.

"Pop the hood," he instructed. "I'll have a look."

She pulled the hood lever, then climbed to the ground while he poked and prodded at several things attached to the engine.

After a few minutes, he finally said, "I don't see anything undone or broken. Which leads me to think you could be right about the problem being with the fuel."

She was already half-frozen from being out in the icy wind. It was growing later by the minute and she was miles and miles from Pioche, the only town in the area large enough to have any sort of amenities for a traveler.

"Well," she said decisively, "I'll have to call a wrecker and have the truck towed to Pioche. Is there a service you'd recommend?"

The glance he flashed her was full of impatience. "By the time a wrecker drove out here and pulled you back to town it would be the wee hours of the morning. And I doubt you'd find a mechanic that would want to crawl out of bed and start repairing your truck at that hour."

Not willing to give in to her dire predicament, she asked, "You don't happen to have a spare vehicle that I could borrow? I'd be happy to pay you for its use."

He slammed the hood shut on the pricey vehicle and walked back over to where she stood. "Just an old truck we use here on the ranch," he explained. "It's not even highway legal."

"Oh. Well, it was just a thought," she said, trying her best not to sound dejected.

"Look, Dallas, I'd offer to drive you in to Pioche, but I'm not about to leave Hayley on the ranch by herself and I'm not going to drag her about for three fourths of the night. Especially when tomorrow is a school day."

She'd not even gotten as far as that solution, Dallas thought. But she could see how the idea of him driving her all the way to Pioche was just as problematic as calling for a wrecker.

She might as well face the fact that she was stranded in the middle of nowhere, without anyone to rely on for help, except this big stone-faced horseman.

"I would never ask you to do such a thing, anyway,"

she told him, then released a short, helpless laugh. "But I am going to ask what you suggest I do now?"

A faint grimace tightened his lips. "The way I see it, you have one choice. And that's to stay here tonight."

Chapter Two

Stay here? With him? Oh, God, nothing about this trip was turning out the way she'd planned, Dallas thought desperately.

"Thanks for the offer, but I'd rather get back to Pioche. I've already interrupted your evening." She couldn't imagine spending the night under the same roof with this man. Even if several rooms separated her from this rancher, she'd still know he was close by. She doubted she'd get a wink of sleep.

"The way I see it, you don't have a choice in the matter."

Her spine stiffened. She didn't like anyone, especially a man, telling her that she'd run out of options. She was a doer, a thinker and a fighter. She didn't just give up on something because it seemed hopeless. Even as a child her parents had bemoaned the fact that Dallas would obstinately refuse to accept the word *no*. Now, years later, she was still slow to accept it.

"I certainly do have a choice," she said primly. "I'll call a wrecker and hitch a ride back into Pioche with him. It won't kill me if it's late in the night when I get there. And if my truck can't be repaired by midmorning, I'll rent one."

His features tightened and Dallas realized it was the most emotion he'd shown since she arrived.

"Look, Dallas, I understand this place doesn't have the luxuries you're probably accustomed to. But it should be comfortable enough for you to bear up for a night or two."

It wasn't exactly sarcasm she heard in his voice, or accusation. He'd merely made a flat statement. As though he knew her inside and out and had already decided she was too soft for his type of life. The idea irked her, but she did her best to keep it hidden. She didn't want to get off on the wrong foot with the man. She'd not driven over a thousand miles to go back home with an empty horse trailer.

Trying not to let irritation show in her voice, she said, "That's not the issue at all."

He continued to look at her and Dallas suddenly realized that Boone was the first man in a long, long time who made her remember that she was every inch a woman, complete with desires and frustrations. The notion jolted her even more than being stranded on this remote ranch with him.

"Really? I get the impression that you're not comfortable with the idea of staying here overnight." He folded his arms against his chest as he studied her with a thoughtful eye. "If you're worried about being alone—

with me—forget it. I may not look like a gentleman, but I am."

It was herself she couldn't trust. Not him. Glad the darkness hid the heat blazing on her cheeks, she said, "I'm not worried about that, either."

"Good. Then you should realize that getting back to Pioche tonight is senseless," he stated. "Might as well stay here and deal with the horses in the morning while you wait for a tow truck."

His suggestion did make sense, Dallas thought. And she supposed she could endure being under this man's roof for one night. God only knew she was exhausted from the long drive and to think of rattling back over all those rough miles to Pioche tonight was enough to make her ache all over.

She shrugged with resignation. "That does sound less complicated. As long as you're sure I won't be a bother to you."

His expression a smooth blank, he moved a step closer. "If you get to be a bother, I'll let you know about it. Do you have any bags with you? Or did you leave them at the hotel?"

Seeing he considered the matter settled, she answered, "They're in the backseat. I didn't take time to unload them at the hotel. Guess that turned out to be a good thing."

After fetching her two leather duffels from the truck, he walked off, leaving Dallas to follow on his heels. As they tromped toward the house, she tried not to think of the night ahead or the predicament she'd gotten herself into.

When they reentered the kitchen, Hayley had already disappeared. With his head, Boone motioned toward an arched doorway.

"Follow me and I'll show you to the room you'll be using," he told her. "You might want to freshen up before we eat."

"Sounds great," she murmured.

The remainder of the house was larger than the impression Dallas had gotten from the outside view. After they passed through a long family room and into a narrow hallway, it seemed like they walked forever. Or perhaps it only felt that way to Dallas because the two of them were alone and she was having all sorts of trouble keeping her gaze off of Boone Barnett's backside.

Good grief, the long drive from New Mexico had done something to her, Dallas thought. It wasn't like she was starved for masculine company. A woman couldn't be starved without first getting hungry. And Allen's deception had practically killed her appetite for romance.

Practically, but not completely. Dallas still dated on occasion and she'd not given up entirely on finding the love of her life. Giving up on anything that was important to her just wasn't in her nature. But men and marriage were things she now viewed in a guarded, practical way.

At one point in her life, she'd planned for her work with horses to only be a part-time career, until she began the full-time job of being a wife and mother. Having a husband and children were the things she really wanted and once she'd gotten engaged to Allen, she was certain her dreams were coming true. She'd been certain of him and his love for her.

Yet she couldn't have been more wrong. Only days before the wedding Allen had come to her with a confession. His desire to marry her had been motivated by his wish to be a part of the Donovan wealth, not by love. He'd told her that his conscience had prevented him from going through with the marriage. And, Dallas supposed, once their engagement had ended, it had been that same "conscience" that had sent Allen running back to an old flame.

Since that humiliating heartbreak, no man had made her heart go pitter patter. That is, until tonight, when she'd met Boone Barnett.

"We keep this room ready," Boone told her as he opened a door to their right, "just in case someone needs or wants to stay a few days here on the ranch. Believe it or not, I've had a few people suggest I turn the ranch into a resort, so that people can come and enjoy the quietness. They don't stop to think that once it became a resort there wouldn't be any quietness around here."

Glad that his voice had interrupted her tumbling thoughts, she said, "Back home, the Diamond D is so busy that sometimes the place feels like a minimetropolis."

He carried her bags over to a double bed covered with a white down comforter. The feather-filled blanket sank as he placed the bags on the edge of the mattress. Dallas longingly imagined her body sinking into the softness and sleep temporarily blotting out her problems.

"Are your riding stables located on the family ranch?" he asked.

Her gaze drifted up to his face and suddenly she was imagining him lying beside her, his big hands reaching for her.

Startled by the erotic image, she quickly glanced away from him and swallowed. "Yes. But there's a ridge of mountain separating them from the main working area of the ranch. So I'm out of the way and the seclusion lets the children pretend they're riding in the Wild West."

"Well, there's no pretending needed here," he said dryly. "This *is* the Wild West."

Dallas would certainly agree. Ever since she'd arrived on Boone's ranch she'd been having all sorts of *wild* thoughts and feelings.

He gestured to a door in the far right corner of the room. "There's a bathroom with a shower. And feel free to use the closet or whatever else you might need."

She said, "Thanks, but I doubt I'll be here long enough to hang up my clothes."

His mouth slanted to a vague smile. "I wouldn't be too quick to say that. Pioche isn't exactly overrun with mechanics and parts-supply shops. In fact, I just know of one."

Even so, she wasn't going to let that keep her stranded. Christmas was less than a week away. Back on the Diamond D decorations would abound in every room of the house and even extend to the horse barns, where large stockings filled with peppermints and licorice and fresh fruit would hang by each stall door for the horses to enjoy during the holiday. Parties would be held for the house staff, ranch hands and office employees. Then later, family and friends would gather for rich food, warm drinks and lively dancing. Christmas was always the best of times on the Diamond D and Dallas had never missed being home for the holidays. Somehow, someway, she had to get back to New Mexico before all the merrymaking started.

Smiling with as much confidence as she could muster, she said, "Let's hope the problem will be easy to fix."

"With vehicles, you never know."

Did she imagine it, or did his brown eyes momentarily slide from her face down the length of her body? Just the idea that he might be looking at her in *that* way sent heat crawling up her neck and onto her face.

You're thirty-two years old, Dallas. Not eighteen. All sorts of men have looked at you "that" way. Boone isn't any different from them. The difference is that you're looking back.

"Uh...the room is lovely," she said with a sudden rush. "I'm sure I'll be quite comfortable."

A quirk of a smile lifted one corner of his mouth. "Glad I could oblige," he said. "So whenever you're finished here, I'll be in the kitchen."

With that, Boone left the small bedroom and once he was out of sight a long breath whooshed from Dallas. *Oh, dear, oh, dear,* she silently moaned. The last thing she needed was to have a breakdown in the middle of nowhere and be forced to stay overnight in a stranger's house, with a man who had enough sex appeal to curl her toes. And for all she knew, he was probably married!

But if her instincts were right, Boone Barnett wasn't some woman's husband. The house simply didn't have that feminine feel about it. And he'd said that Hayley's mother wasn't around. That could only mean the woman had died or lived elsewhere.

Trying to ignore her tumbling thoughts, she slipped out of her jacket, grabbed a hairbrush from one of her bags and headed to the bathroom.

A few short minutes later, she entered the warm kitchen to see Boone placing plates and silverware on the table. As she walked toward him, he glanced up from the simple task to acknowledge her approach.

"I hope you can eat pizza," he said. "We don't always eat fast food, but today has been...hectic."

"Don't worry about me. I eat anything and everything," she replied. She noticed only two plates on the table, and asked, "Won't Hayley be joining us?"

"She mostly eats in her room. And I see three slices of the pizza are missing."

So he and his young daughter didn't usually gather around the table for an evening meal together, Dallas pondered. Was that what happened when there was no mother around to hold things together? Except for Boone, Hayley appeared to be alone. The idea bothered Dallas. During her childhood, she'd been swaddled in love and support from family. And over the years that hadn't changed.

"Is your daughter the only child you have?" The question popped out of Dallas's mouth before she could stop it.

"Yes. Her mother and I divorced when Hayley was only two."

His statement brought Dallas up short. That meant he'd been alone for ten years or so! How had that happened? Even though the population in this area appeared to be scarce, surely there were young women around just waiting for a man to propose matrimony, especially a man that looked like Boone Barnett. But maybe one failed marriage had soured him, she decided. Just like Allen's subterfuge had left her wary of men and doubting she'd ever find one who could really love her.

Trying to turn off her curiosity about this rancher, she watched him carry the pizza over to the table. "Is there anything I can help you with?" she offered.

"No, thanks. I can manage." He pulled out a chair and gestured for her to take a seat. "Just relax. I'll bring the rest over. Is soda okay for you? Or water?"

"Water, please."

While he went to fetch the last of their meal, Dallas

eased down in the wooden dining chair. While she'd been in her room, he'd used the short time to make a salad. Two bottles of dressing and a shaker of Parmesan cheese sat alongside the food. As Dallas looked at the simple meal, she couldn't help thinking how different it was for her family.

The Diamond D had always employed a cook and maids. If anyone came in from a late night of work, he or she didn't have to scrounge up a meal. A substantial plate of dinner would always be left in the warming drawer or the refrigerator. And after it was eaten, there was no need to bother cleaning up the mess. Someone would come by later and take care of the chore.

But Boone wasn't so privileged to have such extensive hired help. He didn't even have a wife to help him with household tasks, much less share the responsibilities of caring for Hayley. The fact that he had any time left to train horses amazed Dallas.

Returning to the table with their drinks, he took a seat directly across from Dallas and she firmly told herself not to think of the quiet supper as anything more than an intake of food.

Carefully avoiding his gaze, she said, "After we eat, I'll call the hotel and let them know I won't be showing up tonight. I had reservations at the old hotel in town— the one with the saloon downstairs below the rooms. I understand it's a favorite with tourists and the locals."

He handed the salad bowl to her. "That's what I hear."

When he didn't elaborate, she could only assume that the establishment wasn't a social spot he frequented. But then she'd already gotten the impression that Boone wasn't the socializing sort.

Ladling a small amount of salad onto her plate, she said, "You were saying earlier that a cell phone won't work out here. Do you mean just for the time being, or do cells never work here on the ranch?"

"I meant never," he answered. "You might get a usable signal in town, depending on the service you use. But even that is iffy. You might be able to send a text message from here. I don't know—I'm not up on that technical sort of stuff."

She offered the bowl of salad to him. "I see. Well, it's mostly like that on our ranch, too," she told him. "We live between mountain ranges and the signal is blocked." Smiling, she shrugged. "When city folks show up on the Diamond D they think they've stepped in the twilight zone. Some people just can't manage life without their technical gadgets. I use them, but on the other hand I can happily exist without them. And sometimes simpler is better. Take my truck, for instance. If the engine wasn't controlled by a computer system, I could probably adjust the carburetor with a screwdriver and be on my way."

As soon as her words died away, she realized she'd been rattling and her cheeks blushed with embarrassment. She opened her mouth to apologize for all the chatter, but immediately pressed her lips back together. She wasn't going to apologize for being herself. Besides, it didn't matter if she was getting on Boone's nerves. He'd already ripped hers to shreds.

For the next few moments they both busied themselves with filling their plates. As they began to eat, Dallas remained quiet and so did Boone.

Eventually, after she'd downed a whole slice of meaty pizza, he decided to speak. "Progress means changes and I don't like changes. I suppose that's why I like living here. It keeps me away from most of it."

There was nothing wrong with being a bit old-fashioned; she was behind the times on some things herself. And if Boone chose to live that way, that was his business. After all, he was a grown man. But it was a different situation with Hayley. As a child, she probably had no say in the matter, and Dallas couldn't help but wonder how the young girl felt about living in such a secluded way. Surely Hayley missed doing the typical things that tweens and teens enjoyed, like calling and texting friends or spending the evening at the mall or the cinema.

Even though Dallas had grown up in the country and understood what it was like to live without the lights and excitement of town, she'd not been nearly as isolated as Hayley. Getting from the Diamond D to civilization was easy compared to the trip between Pioche and White River Ranch. Plus, she'd had siblings and neighboring friends no more than three miles away. Clearly, the distance between Hayley and her friends had to be much greater.

"Carburetors haven't been around for years," he said after a moment. "You're too young to know about such things."

His remarks interrupted her thoughts about Hayley and she was glad. Questions about this man and his daughter were beginning to consume her and that couldn't be good. Once she left Nevada their paths would most likely never cross again.

Smiling vaguely, she said, "I'm thirty-two—that's not so young. And the mechanics—well, I've always been a bit of a tomboy and the man who repairs the old trucks and tractors on our ranch is like a granddad to me. When I was around Hayley's age, I'd trail along with him just to hear him tell stories—not about machinery, but about horses. I guess I digested more about motors than I realized."

He cast a thoughtful glance at her. "Is running the stables your only job?"

Was he actually curious about her, Dallas wondered, or simply trying to maintain a conversation? Either way, she was surprised he was bothering to ask questions.

She said, "My younger sister is a doctor and my older sister a nurse. I've been asked a jillion times why I didn't follow them into a medical field. But that's not me. Nothing outside the ranch is me, I guess. I have a degree in livestock- and land-management. But the one thing I'm truly good at is horses. Pitiful, isn't it?"

For the first time since she'd met him, the corners of his mouth turned upward enough to constitute a genuine smile. The sight of it was like a ray of sunshine melting right through her. Oh, dear, the man was doing something to her and he wasn't even trying, she thought desperately.

"I wouldn't call you...pitiful."

Her mouth like cotton, she reached for her water glass. The crystal clear liquid had a faint metallic taste, as though it had come from deep within the ground. And she supposed it had. During the twenty-mile trip out here, she'd not spotted any creeks or rivers. Only windmills. It was a harsh land toiled by an even tougher man, she decided.

"Well," she said, "blame my lack of outside interest on my father. By the time I was old enough to walk he had me down at the barns and exercise track. For years, I didn't know life beyond the four-legged creatures existed. And by the time I was old enough to realize there were other things in the world, I wasn't interested in pursuing any of them."

His head bent over his plate, but not before she saw the corners of his mouth turn downward. "You told Hayley that you didn't have a husband or kids. Is that true?"

Two years, or even a year ago, his question would have filled her with pain and an utter sense of loss. Now she was stronger. Now she could think of Allen and thank God that she'd not made the horrible mistake of marrying him.

"It's hard for a tall girl to get a date," she joked, then when he didn't appear to be amused, she added in a more sober tone, "Seriously, the right man just hasn't come along. I came close to marrying once but he... Well, that didn't work out. And since then most of the men I've dated always ended up trying to pull me away from the ranch and what I do. And I end up pulling back. A tug-of-war tears people and marriages apart. I'm smart enough to know that."

Lifting his gaze to hers, he said softly, "Yes. I believe you are just that—smart."

Even though his face was impossible to read, she could tell from his voice that he'd meant the comment as a compliment. Though she didn't know why, the idea was ridiculously pleasing to her.

As Boone watched Dallas fork a morsel of food to her mouth, he couldn't help thinking how the day had turned out to be a strange one. First thing this morning, he'd found a mama-to-be cat in the barn. Since he had no cats and his nearest neighbor was at least ten miles away, he didn't know where she'd come from or how she'd gotten to the ranch. In any case, she'd made herself at home and trotted along behind him as though she was certain he was going to be more than happy to be her master. And then his old ranch horse, the gelding he'd had for more than fifteen years—the one who was so ill-natured he kicked or bit any four-legged creature that happened to come near his end of the feed trough—had eaten his breakfast snuggled up to a mustang mare, as though he'd found himself a little angel. Now here Boone was sitting at the supper table with a *woman*.

What were the chances of a new truck going on the blink? he asked himself. Damn little to none, that's how many. And if someone had told him a woman with pretty red hair and a soft smile would be warming up his kitchen tonight, he'd have declared the person crazy. Yeah, the day had been unusual, he decided. And the night was just starting.

"How long have you lived on this ranch?" she asked.

For a moment his gaze was caught on her lips and the way the plush curves moved as they formed words. The gentle tilt at the corners of her mouth implied she was constantly smiling and he tried to imagine what it might be like to live with a woman like her, a woman who wasn't staring at him with vacant eyes and an expression of utter detachment.

She's not Joan. But she could still cause you a ton of trouble. Especially if you don't get your eyes off her lips and your mind back to business.

Boone shifted in his seat. "Ever since I was born—thirty-nine years ago."

"That's a long time," she replied, then laughed contritely. "Sorry. I didn't mean to imply that you're old. I just meant that thirty-nine years is a long time for anyone to be in one spot."

"You've stayed in the same spot all your life. Or so you said," he pointed out, while thinking it had been ages and ages since he'd had a conversation like this with a woman.

There were occasional times, when his father was sober enough to have Hayley visit, or when she stayed overnight with friends, that Boone would go into town for a beer and a willing woman. But those instances were not just rare, they were different. This woman was different.

"That's true. I have lived my whole life on the Diamond D," she admitted. "And I don't plan to leave it, either."

The last statement she said with conviction and Boone tended to believe what she said. After all, she was thirty-two and still living on the ranch. Obviously no man had been able to pull her away. He liked that about her and the fact that she had an independent streak. Even more, she seemed confident about the things she wanted. Too bad Joan hadn't been that strong and decisive. His ex-wife had never known what, if anything, could make her happy. At one time, she'd believed her happiness lay solely in Boone. But she'd been confused about him and this life he'd chosen to lead; just as she'd been confused about her own life and where she fit in this world.

Biting back a sigh of regret, he said, "My grandparents purchased this stretch of range when my father was a young teenager—just a bit older than Hayley. Before then, Granddad worked in the silver mines. But he'd come from a ranching family down in Arizona and that way of life was in his blood. He took what money he'd managed to save over the years and sank it into this place. And for the past decade I've leased four hundred thousand acres of public land to go with it for extra grazing."

Boone stabbed his fork into the pizza on his plate and wondered what the hell had prompted him to say all those things. Normally he never talked about his past or his family. And he especially didn't share such personal things with horse buyers. But for some reason Dallas felt like more than a visiting horse buyer. Maybe that was because she was continuing to study him with genuine interest. Or had it been so long since he'd spent time with a woman that he was reading Dallas all wrong?

"What about your father?" she asked. "He's not a rancher?"

The thought of Newt Barnett was enough to cause Boone to clench his teeth. The man had always been a sponger, and for the most part had ignored his responsibilities as a father, a husband and even as a son. He'd squandered and drank and whined through most of his life. And yet Newt expected Boone to forgive his mistakes and show him the love and respect of a father. Boone had never wanted to think of himself as a hardhearted person, but Newt was yet to give him one good reason to love and respect him.

"Ranching is hard work," Boone said flatly. "Newt has always wanted things the easy way."

Dallas's hand fluttered up to her throat and Boone could see his statement had disturbed her. He probably shouldn't have been so blunt. But Boone never was one to sugarcoat anything and he sure as hell wasn't going to try to pretend his father was a respectable, productive citizen of Lincoln County. Not even to impress this lady.

"You sound—" her gaze dropped awkwardly to her plate "—as though the two of you don't get along very well."

"We never have," he admitted. "But that's a whole other story."

Several awkward moments passed in silence and then she said, "My grandparents emigrated from Ireland and first settled in Kentucky. But by the 1960s, Grandfather Arthur got the urge to travel west and acquire more land. He fell in love with New Mexico and decided it was the perfect place to raise his Thoroughbreds. Out of two daughters and a son, Dad was the only child who stayed in the business and kept the ranch going." She cast a wry glance at him, as though she wasn't sure she should ask her next question. "Where are your grandparents now?"

His dark brown eyes flickered with raw emotions and Dallas realized he wasn't the indifferent cowboy she'd first believed him to be.

"Dead," he said bluntly. "They'd gone on a hunting trip and the small aircraft they were traveling in hit an ice storm over the Montana plains and crashed. They were only in their fifties at the time. I was just fifteen and it... Well, it took me a long time to accept that the both of them were really gone. When you're young you think you'll have your loved ones around forever."

Somewhere in his husky voice Dallas could hear his loss and the idea of Boone going through such a tragedy thickened her throat and tangled her usually ready words. "You must have been...utterly crushed."

He looked away from her. "Yeah, crushed was right. You see, from the time I was a little toddler, they'd basically been my parents." Shrugging, he brought his gaze back to hers. "But things happen and life goes on."

She wanted to ask more. Like why had his grandparents been raising him and what had happened after their death, but the temptation to question him further was suddenly interrupted as he rose to his feet and walked over to the cabinet.

"Hayley made cookies yesterday," he said from across the room. "I guess they'll have to do for dessert. I'll make fresh coffee to go with them."

Since he appeared to be finished with his meal, Dallas downed her last bite and gathered up their dirty plates. As she placed them on the cabinet counter, her gaze swept over the varnished pine cabinets and white appliances. Even though there was a bit of clutter here and there, everything was very clean. Did Hayley help him with the kitchen cleaning chores? Or maybe he had a cleaning woman come in at different times during the week.

Quit pretending, Dallas. You're not wondering about a cleaning woman. You're wondering about Boone having a woman in his life.

Annoyed with herself and the tacky voice chiming from somewhere inside of her, she walked back over to the table and began to gather up the remainder of the meal.

This was not the way her trip was supposed to be going, she thought with a bit of desperation. She'd come here with plans to buy horses. Not to be trapped on a ranch with a man who was quickly and surely starting to consume her every thought.

She had to get a grip and remember that the only stud she was looking for was the four-legged kind. But each time her gaze rested on Boone she had difficulty remembering anything—except that she was a woman and he was one very unforgettable man.

And the night had only begun.

Chapter Three

"Don't bother with that," Boone said as she carried an armful of dishes across the room. "Hayley will deal with it later."

"I don't mind," she insisted. "It's the least I can do for you so graciously putting me up tonight."

While the coffee brewed, Dallas scraped the dishes and stacked them to one side of the porcelain sink. Just to her right, Boone pulled a lid from a plastic container and placed several cookies on a paper plate.

For some reason, standing near him like this, doing domestic chores together, felt even more intimate than when he was showing her the bedroom. Although she tried to ignore it, her heart was going at a fast clip and she feared her cheeks were flushed with color.

"If you'd like, we can take this in the family room," he suggested. "You can use the phone in there."

Clearing her throat, she was quick to agree. "Sounds good to me."

After he placed the coffee and the cookies on a plastic tray, she followed him out of the kitchen and down to the family room. As she took in the simply furnished area, she noticed a huge fireplace took up the major part of one wall. A warm welcoming fire would have gone a long way in brightening the room, but presently the hearth was cold and dark.

As if he could read her thoughts, he said, "I've cleared away most of the underbrush on the ranch and there's not much left to burn. To have a fire every evening, I'd have to drive up to Ely and buy firewood, so I've been rationing until my next trip."

"And I'm sure it's expensive," she stated.

"Very."

He gestured to a long green sofa and matching armchair. "Have a seat anywhere you'd like. The phone is there at the end of the sofa."

"Thanks." She sank down on the sofa, then reached for the phone and directory resting beneath it.

After a quick explanation to the hotel clerk, Dallas placed the receiver back on its hook, then helped herself to the coffee and cookies that Boone had left on the table in front of her.

"If you need to call your family—or anyone—to let them know you arrived safely, please do."

Dallas looked over to see he'd settled comfortably back in the chair and crossed his ankles out in front of him. The jeans covering his long, muscled legs were faded nearly white, the hems slightly frayed. His snub-toed cowboy boots had once been brown roughout leather, but were now smooth and dark from countless hours of wear. Dallas doubted he'd ever seen the inside of a department store or mall and if he had, he'd gone there reluctantly. Still, he was the perfect image for a jeans commercial. An idea he'd no doubt laugh at, she thought.

"I called my family when I first arrived at Pioche. So they know I've made the trip safely. Right now I don't want to worry Liam needlessly about the truck. At least, not until I can give him an exact problem."

Boone said, "I hope he wasn't planning on using the truck anytime soon."

Dallas darted him a sharp glance. He made it sound like getting her vehicle running again was going to take days instead of hours. Oh, God, that couldn't happen. She couldn't spend days with this man. It would wreck her!

Trying not to think the worst, she replied, "Most of the tracks on the West Coast won't be having any major races to speak of until after the New Year. So my brother won't be doing much traveling. That's one of the reasons why I planned the trip for this month. Plus with Christmas coming up, many of my kids won't be visiting the stables. They're involved with family holiday things right now."

From the moment she'd arrived on the ranch, Dallas had noticed there were no holiday decorations to be seen in or out of the Barnett house. Maybe they practiced some sort of religion that didn't celebrate Christmas, she thought, as she munched on an oatmeal-and-raisin cookie. But she seriously doubted that was the reason for the lack of festiveness. She was more inclined to think that Boone had forgotten how to celebrate anything.

"Are your stables closed while you're away?" he asked.

"No. My sister-in-law, Lass, is my assistant and she's keeping the place running for the few children who do show up."

Earlier today, when Dallas had called home, her

mother had given her breaking family news that
amounted to a double whammy. At breakfast this morning Lass and Brady had revealed they were expecting a
second child and before they'd hardly gotten the words
out of their mouths, Bridget and Johnny had announced
their first child was on its way. In a few months two
babies would be arriving in the Donovan family at the
same time. Dallas was thrilled for her brother and her
sister, yet somehow the news had left her feeling a bit
melancholy. She was already thirty-two. Would there
ever come a day, she wondered, when she would become
a mother? It didn't seem likely. Not when the idea of
giving her heart to another man made her want to turn
tail and run.

Not wanting to dwell on that miserable thought, she
turned her gaze back on Boone to see he was studying
her with those dark, brooding eyes. Did he ever think
about having a baby with another woman? The notion
bothered her in more ways than she wanted to admit.

Swallowing to ease the tightness in her throat, she
asked, "Do you have hired help on your ranch? Or do
you do it all yourself?"

"I have a man who comes in three or four days a week
to help with the ranch work. Depending on what's going
on."

On the opposite side of the room, directly across from
the couch, there was a small television. Presently the
screen was black, a status that didn't surprise Dallas. In
fact, she couldn't imagine this rugged cowboy sitting
down to watch a drama or sitcom. Maybe the news. But
nothing for the sole purpose of entertainment.

She was still speculating as to what he'd consider entertainment when the telephone beside her suddenly rang.

The unexpected sound caused her to flinch and her head jerked toward the jangling instrument.

Making no move to answer it, he said, "Hayley will pick it up. It's usually for her, anyway. You know how it is with kids."

There was that subject again. Kids, children, babies. Normally she didn't dwell on her single status. But something about Boone and his daughter, coupled with the news of Lass's and Bridget's pregnancies, had gotten to her, making her want to weep and scream at the same time.

Biting back a sigh, she gave him a wan smile. "I imagine you—"

Her comment was cut short as Hayley suddenly yelled from somewhere in the hallway. "Dad! It's for you! Can you pick up the phone?"

"Who's calling?"

The girl came trotting into the room, carrying a portable phone with her hand clamped tightly over the receiver. She started toward Boone, then stopped short when she spotted Dallas on the couch.

Her face a mixture of perplexed pleasure, she said, "Oh! Dallas! I thought you'd left."

Dallas smiled at her. "I thought I was leaving, too. But my truck decided to call it quits."

"Hayley, the phone. Who is it?"

Boone's question jerked the girl's attention back to her father. "It's Billy Hopper. Something about welding on the hay loader."

"Excuse me, Dallas," he said, then quickly rose to his feet, took the phone from Hayley and exited the room.

Once her father was out of sight, Hayley walked over to the sofa and sank onto the edge of the cushion next to Dallas.

"What are you gonna do now?" she asked curiously. "Is Dad gonna drive you to Pioche tonight?"

Dallas shook her head. "No. I'm going to stay here for the night. I hope you don't mind," she added. "Your father assured me that you sometimes have guests on the ranch."

Hayley's features suddenly perked with interest. "Uh—we've had a few, but they've all been old men. But…well…gosh, it'll be nice to have you stay!"

Dallas smiled with relief. "I'm glad you feel that way."

Her eyes sparkling, Hayley scooted closer to Dallas. "Earlier, when you said goodbye I was wishing you could stay longer. I've never seen anybody as pretty as you. And I wanted to ask you what it's like where you live and things like that. Would you care to tell me?"

She'd never expected such an endearing reaction from Hayley. In fact, she'd thought the girl would probably resent the intrusion of having a guest in the house.

"Thank you for the compliment, Hayley, but I'm just average-looking. I have two sisters who are much prettier than I am."

"Wow, you have two sisters?" she asked, then like a switch had been flipped, her expression turned glum. "I wish I had a sister or even a brother. But I guess all I'll ever have is just me."

Dallas let out a silent groan. Babies. She just couldn't get away from the subject tonight.

"Your father is still young," Dallas said with as much encouragement as she could muster. "He might marry again and have more children."

Shaking her head, Hayley leaned toward Dallas and lowered her voice. "Dad wouldn't like it if he heard me talking about this kind of stuff. And I don't ever—but you're a grown-up woman and I don't get to talk to anybody like you."

Dallas was perplexed. "What about your friends? Surely they have mothers you can talk with?"

The girl wrinkled up her nose. "I don't trust any of them. They're all friends of my dad's and whatever I said might get back to him. And then I'd be grounded for weeks."

"Oh. I see." Dallas reached over and patted the girl's hand. "Well, for what it's worth, you can trust me. I'll keep our conversation in confidence."

Sighing with relief, Hayley quickly leaned closer and lowered her voice another notch. "Well, the reason I don't think I'll ever get a brother or sister is 'cause Dad doesn't want to ever get married again. Because my mother was so awful. And he says that so many years would be between me and a little brother or sister that we most likely wouldn't be close. But I believe we would. Dad just uses that for an excuse. And it's a dumb one."

Dallas ached for this young girl with sad brown eyes and a wish in her heart to belong to a whole family. "Do you see your mother often?"

Hayley shot her a puzzled, almost comical look. "Often? Shoot, I never see her. Dad says I was three the last time she came around. But I don't remember it."

Dazed by what she was hearing, Dallas hardly knew how to respond to this girl who seemed so hungry for female guidance. "I'm sorry, Hayley. That must be rough."

The girl shrugged one shoulder as though to say she wasn't bothered by the fact. But Dallas could see that being abandoned by her mother had obviously had a profound effect on the child.

Hayley said, "I don't sweat it that much. I mean, I

don't remember her, so there's not a lot for me to miss. Dad says she had psychological problems and had to live in a mental clinic for a while. Now I guess she's well enough. She's married to someone else. Once in a while I get a postcard from her. But that's about it."

Oh, God, what kind of woman could simply walk away from her own daughter? A woman who had some sort of mental or emotional breakdown, Dallas realized. But if she'd gotten well enough to remarry, what was her reason for staying away from Hayley now? Boone? No. Dallas couldn't imagine him keeping his ex-wife away from their daughter just for spiteful reasons.

"So your mother didn't have any more children?" Dallas asked while trying to tell herself she wasn't prying. Hayley clearly needed to talk and it wasn't like Dallas was going to take the information and spread it.

Dropping her head in a guilty manner, Hayley mumbled, "No. Something happened after I was born and she couldn't have more kids. That's what my grandma Elsa told me once." Turning a wistful expression on Dallas, she asked, "Do you have a nice mother?"

Hayley's ingenuous question caused tears to sting the back of Dallas's eyes. "Yes. She's a wonderful mother. Her name is Fiona. And my grandmother, Kate, lives with us, too. And I have three brothers, also."

"Boy, your house must be full of people."

"Most of the time it is." Dallas reached for another cookie. "Your father said you baked these. They're delicious."

Hayley shrugged again. "Cookies are no big deal. I've been making them for a long time. I'm learning to cook whole meals now. Dad says I'm doing good. But sometimes I burn things."

At Hayley's age, Dallas had hated doing anything in

the kitchen, and she still wasn't all that good at putting a meal together. Clearly Hayley wasn't nearly as much of a tomboy as Dallas had been.

"You like to cook?" she asked the girl.

"Sure. There's not much else to do around here. And I like helping Dad. He works so hard. With the horses and all. And he never spends any money on himself. He's saving it all for me. So that I can go to college. I wish he wouldn't do that. But he won't listen to me," she said, ending her declaration with an exaggerated sigh. "I guess dads are just like that."

Yes, the good ones, Dallas thought. And she was beginning to see that Boone was one of the good ones. He might not understand all of Hayley's feminine needs, but he obviously was making sure her home and future were secure.

"My father worked hard and sacrificed for his children, too," she told the girl.

"What does he do?"

"He's mostly retired now. But he raises Thoroughbred horses and races them. Do you know what they are?"

Her eyes suddenly glowing, Hayley bobbed her head and Dallas decided this was the first real excitement she'd seen on the girl's face.

"Oh, yeah! One time we went to Elko to the fair. They were having races and we went to the paddock and watched them saddle the Thoroughbreds. They were so big and beautiful and I told Dad we should get some. But he said we wouldn't have any use for those kinds of horses on the ranch. He said they were only for running fast." Hayley gave her eyes an impatient roll. "He should know that some of us like to run fast just for the fun of it. Don't you?"

Dallas found it impossible to hide her smile. Especially when she could easily recall how it was to be Hayley's age, to swing upon a horse's back and race across the open field with the wind blowing in her face and the rush of exhilaration humming through her. There had been countless occasions when her father, Doyle, had admonished Dallas for riding recklessly. But she'd been young and fierce then. Just the way she suspected Hayley was now.

"Yes, I do like to go fast," Dallas admitted, "and Thoroughbreds are good at other jobs, too. But I'm sure the mustangs your father have are equally nice—in different ways."

Hayley's nose wrinkled as she considered Dallas's diplomatic statement. "Well, most of them are smart," she agreed. "And Dad says that not everything has to be beautiful to be worth something."

During her teenage years and beyond, Dallas had often felt overshadowed by her lovely sisters. They were both petite women with soft, feminine appearances. Dallas had always thought of herself as the big, coarse Donovan sister. But thankfully she'd grown beyond those foolish thoughts and learned that true beauty had nothing to do with the outside and everything to do with the heart.

"I think your Dad is a very wise man," Dallas said gently and was surprised at how very much she meant it.

While Hayley's gaze dropped uncomfortably to her lap, Dallas noticed the bright pink polish on the girl's fingernails was terribly chipped and the elastic in her beaded bracelet frayed. Did the girl get any maternal guidance? Dallas wondered. The mother was obviously out of the picture and Boone had only mentioned having his father, so that meant his mother was either dead or moved away. From what Hayley had told her earlier, there didn't seem to be any other woman around that she felt comfortable talking to. The idea bothered Dallas greatly.

"Yeah, but sometimes he just doesn't get it," she mumbled. "He doesn't understand what it's like to be a girl."

Chuckling softly, Dallas did her best to keep the moment light. "Don't feel badly. My dad has never understood girl stuff, either."

Hayley looked up and a tiny semblance of a smile curved her mouth. "I'd better go. It's my night to wash dishes." She jumped to her feet. "I wouldn't bother waiting around on Dad to get off the phone. Billy is a big talker."

Well, it wasn't as if Boone was supposed to hang around and keep her entertained, Dallas thought. In fact, it was probably a good thing that business had called him away. The break had given her a chance to catch her breath and remember why she'd ever come to this ranch in the first place.

Hayley pointed to a remote control lying on a table near the armchair. "Watch TV if you like. We only get three channels, but I guess that's better than nothing. We have a few movies for the DVD player, but they're mostly old."

Plucking up her coffee mug, Dallas rose from the sofa. "Why don't I just help you with the dishes?" she suggested. "That sounds like more fun to me."

Hayley was amazed. "Really?"

Laughing, Dallas motioned toward the open doorway. "Sure. Lead the way."

Fifteen minutes later, Boone entered the kitchen just as Hayley was washing the last plate and Dallas was putting silverware away in a drawer. For a moment the domestic sight brought him up short. Since his mother,

Elsa, had passed away, there had been no adult women in the house. Seeing Dallas working side by side with his daughter was a blunt reminder of all the things that Hayley was missing, all the things she needed that he couldn't provide.

Moving deeper into the room, he asked, "Since when do we put a guest to work, Hayley?"

"Don't blame her," Dallas quickly defended. "I wanted to help."

"That's right, Dad," Hayley added for good measure. "And it would have been rude for me to refuse."

Hayley looked over to Dallas and the two of them exchanged conspiring grins. Boone was totally surprised at his daughter's sudden change in attitude. Normally, getting a smile out of her was like pulling a tooth. She'd never been one to take to strangers, particularly women. The mistrust of females had something to do with her mother deserting her, Boone figured. But tonight he couldn't see a drop of wariness toward Dallas. And he didn't know whether to be glad or worried about this sudden bond she'd developed with Dallas. More than likely the woman would be gone tomorrow. Hayley needed to remember that their guest was just that—a temporary guest.

He walked over to Hayley. "Okay, but you'd better finish up here and get to bed," he told his daughter. "Tomorrow is a school day, remember?"

"Aw, Dad, how could I forget? It's only Wednesday!" Once again she glanced at Dallas. "And I haven't finished my math assignment. Dallas says she'll help me with my homework."

Totally bewildered now, Boone looked over at the woman, who'd quickly made herself at home in his house and with his daughter.

"I thought you said you had your own problems with math."

He might have imagined it, but Dallas's shoulders seem to draw up and her back straighten.

"You misunderstood. I said I didn't like it," she politely corrected. "But once my parents explained exactly how important math was, I studied hard and changed that D into A's."

He couldn't argue with that, Boone decided. And why would he want to? For the first time, in a long, long time his daughter was showing interest in something other than talking on the phone or holing up in her room with a CD player blasting music.

"All right," he said to Dallas. To his daughter, he slanted a pointed look. "I expect you to be in bed in forty minutes. No more."

Heaving out a relieved breath, Hayley flashed a smile at Dallas. "I promise, Dad."

Close to an hour later, Boone was sitting at a rolltop desk that was situated in an out-of-the-way corner of the kitchen, entering monthly expenditures into the ranch's bookkeeping ledger. Usually at this late hour, he was in bed, or at the very least, retired to his bedroom to read. But tonight, with a guest in the house, he'd decided to stay up until he was certain she no longer needed anything.

"Oh. Excuse me."

The sound of Dallas's voice made him jerk his head up and he glanced over his shoulder to see she was standing just inside the doorway. She'd changed into blue pajamas and a robe and though the garments covered every inch of her, they still looked like bedclothes, a thought that sent his senses into overdrive and left him gawking like a teenager.

As though she could read his thoughts, she clutched the collar of her pajamas to her throat. "I didn't mean to disturb you. I just needed a drink of water. To take a pill." She held up the caplet for him to see. "My bossy doctor sister would have my hide if I didn't take it."

Twisting the swivel chair so that he was facing her, Boone gestured to the refrigerator. "Help yourself. You'll find a container of chilled water in the fridge."

She walked over to the cabinet, pulled down a small juice glass, then stepped over to the refrigerator. As Boone watched her movements he tried to remember the last time he'd felt this physically attracted to woman, but try as he might he couldn't recall any woman affecting his senses this much.

"You have...a health problem?" Hell, for all he knew that pill squeezed between her fingers could be birth control, he silently cursed. The notion made the stirring in his loins even more uncomfortable. "Sorry, that's none of my business."

She took a moment to swallow the pill, then replied, "No major health problems. I just need a little extra iron." Chuckling, she used one hand to motion down her body. "Doesn't look like I'd have that problem, does it? I take after my grandma Kate, I look as stout as a horse."

Boone could have told her that she looked incredibly healthy, vibrant and beautiful to him. But he never said such words to any woman. Once, long ago, he'd said flowery things to Joan, things that he'd thought his wife had wanted and needed to hear. Unfortunately, the words had simply gone into one ear and out the other. She'd been too lost in her own private misery to grasp much of what anyone said to her. Now, so many years had passed since then that Boone doubted he could have that sort of intimate conversation with a woman.

"That's good," he said awkwardly. "That your health is…good."

Leaning a hip against the cabinet counter, she folded her arms loosely around her waist and suddenly Boone was wondering what she would look like beneath all those thick bedclothes. Would the rest of her skin look as creamy as her face, would her breasts be full and the nipples pale pink?

Hell, Boone. Hell, hell! What are you thinking? She isn't your style. She's way out of your league. She'll be gone soon.

And if those three reasons weren't enough to steer clear of the woman, Boone thought, there was one more. And it was probably the most important reason of all. She was a good woman. Not a woman to take to his bed.

"I want you to know I enjoyed Hayley's company tonight," she said. "She's a lovely child and very bright. You must be so proud of her."

The mention of his daughter was enough to dampen his erotic thoughts, at least for the moment.

"It's not always been easy raising her," he admitted. "Hayley was only two when Joan left us. And up until then the most I'd ever done was hold a bottle to her mouth or change her diaper. Mom tried to help as best she could, but she always had her hands more than full with Dad. I guess you could say with me and Hayley it was one of those learn as you go things."

Even with a few feet separating them, he could see curiosity in her eyes and he wondered if she was viewing his life as some sort of badly written soap opera.

If so, she wouldn't be far off, Boone thought wryly. The Barnetts had never been what most people considered normal folks. His family had all the key ingredients for a continuing saga: tragedy, desertions, addictions and heartaches. Oh, yes, Boone's dour thoughts continued, there'd been plenty of drama, heartaches and loneliness.

"Your mother isn't with you anymore?" she asked gently.

Tossing the pencil onto a stack of statements, he raked a hand through his hair. He didn't much like talking about his mother. Not that he hadn't loved Elsa Barnett. He had. But her love and loyalty had always been directed at her worthless husband. Boone had only gotten the scraps of her affection. Still, she'd tried to do the best she could for her son and that had been far more than Joan had ever managed to do for Hayley.

"My mom died of a heart attack about five years ago. Since then, Dad's drinking has gotten a whole lot worse. He blames himself for her death."

"Should he?"

Biting back a sigh, Boone swiped a weary hand over his face. Thinking about his parents, about the years his father had wasted—even worse, the years his mother had lost while she waited for her husband to turn into an upright human being—always left him feeling cold and empty.

"I'll put it this way. If I were in his shoes, I wouldn't find it easy to live with myself."

"Oh. Sorry."

He frowned at her. "You've been saying that to me a lot this evening. You must be thinking I have a miserable life and family."

Surprise widened her eyes. "Oh. I'm sorry," she said again, and then blushing with embarrassment, she shook her head. "Forgive me, Boone. I've not been thinking anything like that. I...actually, I've been thinking how different your life is from mine. I mean, things haven't always been perfect for me, either. And I wish—well, I wish that some things could have been better for you. That's all."

Switching off the lamp on the desk, he rose to his feet and walked over to where she stood with her back resting against the cabinet counter. The scent of flowers drifted to him and lured his senses like a sweet, soft whisper.

"You're way off base, Dallas, if you're feeling sorry for me."

Suddenly she tossed her head back and not for the first time since she'd walked into the room, Boone noticed that she'd brushed her hair and the tresses now waved thickly and wildly upon her shoulders. Funny, how his fingers were suddenly tingling to touch and slide against all that silkiness.

"That," she said succinctly, "is not what I meant at all."

"No?" he asked, his voice going deceptively soft. "Then what did you mean?"

Even though the outside of the man was as tough as rawhide, Dallas could plainly see there were sensitive spots underneath. And somehow she'd unwittingly managed to rub those spots the wrong way.

A shiver hit the base of her neck, then slid down her spine. He was so close she could see the light and dark flecks in his brown eyes, the pores in his tanned skin, and oh, so tempting curve of his lips. What was he doing getting this close, she wondered. And why was a part of her wanting him to get even closer?

"Look, we don't really know each other," she said, trying desperately to hang on to her slipping composure. "But I can see you're a big, strong guy, fully capable of dealing with whatever life throws at you. Compared to the children that frequent my riding stables, you're a very, very blessed man. Maybe you ought to remember that whenever you're stroking that chip on your shoulder."

Faint amusement curved one corner of his lips and Dallas inwardly groaned at the sudden and charming change it brought to his face. The man was disarmingly sexy, she couldn't deny that. And she was succumbing to him like a flower wilting in the desert sun.

"You might call that a chip," he said. "I call it life."

A ragged breath slipped past her lips. "And you think that's something I don't know about? For your information, rich people have heartaches, too. I had to watch my beloved grandfather die from a massive stroke. My sister-in-law and the child she was carrying were killed in a car crash. Now my brother goes around acting as though nothing is wrong when everyone knows he's miserable. One of my sisters was married to a cheating creep and my other brother's first wife had a mental breakdown and I—"

She broke off suddenly, dismayed that she'd allowed herself to pour out such things to him. A few more seconds and she would have been telling him about Allen and how he'd nearly suckered her into a loveless marriage, how he'd only wanted her money and how in the end he'd only fessed up because he couldn't give up the woman he'd really loved. God, what was she thinking? That was a humiliation she didn't talk about to anyone, much less a man she'd only met a few hours ago.

Pushing away from the cabinet she started to move past him and leave the room, but his hand snaked out and caught her by the arm. Stunned by the unexpected touch, she stared at him, and suddenly her heart was beating so fast she could feel it thumping in her throat, and pounding blood at her temples.

"You didn't finish," he said gently.

To be this close to the man was like standing next to a flame, she thought. Heat was roaring off him, burning her face, searing every nerve in her body. She could feel the intensity of his dark gaze as it slid ever so slowly across her cheeks and lips, down her throat, then back up to meet her eyes.

"I don't need to finish," she said stiffly while trying to cool the rapid meltdown going on inside of her. "I shouldn't have gone off like that in the first place."

This time he actually gave her a full-blown grin and for a few spectacular moments she felt everything inside her come to a jarring halt.

"Well," he replied, "I'm glad to see you're not sorry—again."

The moment his hand had touched her arm, the whole room had seemed to alter from a simple kitchen to a dark, forbidden territory. And something about Boone had changed, too. A subtle softening had eased his jaw and lowered his eyelids to seductive slits. To Dallas everything about him spelled sex.

"I think it's time I…go to my room."

"You're probably right," he murmured, "but there's something I should do before you go."

Her lips parted to ask him what that "something" might be. But he didn't give her the chance to form the question. Still holding her arm, he tugged her slightly forward. Teetering on her feet, she thrust out her hands to prevent herself from falling straight into his arms. Her palms splattered against his broad chest and then the next thing she knew, his fingers were beneath her chin, and his lips settling softly over hers.

If she'd had time to anticipate his intentions, she might have escaped. But he'd not given her a moment's chance and even if he had, she doubted she would have found the will to avoid his kiss.

She certainly couldn't find it now as the taste of him

flooded her senses, commanded her thoughts to focus on him and only him.

Beneath the thick fabric of his shirt, the heat of his hard chest seeped into her palms. Scents of alfalfa, horses and man swirled together and filled her nostrils. Yet it was the consuming exploration of his lips that flung her senses straight up to the ceiling.

On and on the kiss went, or so it seemed to Dallas. And then his head suddenly lifted, putting an end to the mating of their lips. Dallas forced her eyelids to open and her gaze to focus on his face.

"Um—what was that?" she finally managed to ask.

The subtle twist of his lips caused her breath to catch, and she curled her fingers into her palms.

"A welcome to the White River Ranch."

Her cheeks flamed with embarrassment. Not because he'd kissed her, but because she'd kissed him back.

"Oh. Is that the sort of welcome you generally give your guests?"

He chuckled and the sound was almost as rich and reckless as his kiss had been. She resisted the urge to press the back of her hand against her burning lips.

"No. But the guests I get out here don't generally look like you."

"Maybe you ought to get out more," she suggested. "You must be starved for the sight of a woman."

His face suddenly serious, he reached out and captured a strand of red hair lying near her breast. Dallas tried not to shiver as he tested its silky texture between the calloused pads of his fingertips.

"I'm starved for…a lot of things, Dallas."

And so was she. That's why she had to escape the circle of his arms before she started clinging to him, begging him to kiss her one more time.

"Good night, Boone."

As soon as she whispered the words, he dropped his hold on her hair and stepped back. Dallas didn't let herself linger, even for a moment. She whirled and ran from him.

Chapter Four

The next morning Dallas awoke to see sunlight streaming through the bedroom window, slanting pale shafts of light across the end of the bed.

Oh, Lord, she'd slept past daylight! A good horseman never let that happen. Their work started early and ended late. No doubt Boone had been waiting for her and thinking the worst! Probably that she was the pampered sort who lounged in bed while the hired hands did all the work. Or even worse, he was thinking she was lying in bed in hopes that he would come to her room and take up where he'd left off last night.

Groaning with dismay, she flung back the covers and leapt from the warm bed. She didn't have time to think about Boone's kiss. Nor did she want to. Reliving it over and over in her mind for half the night was more than enough to make her feel like a sleep-deprived zombie this morning.

Besides, she didn't need to continue analyzing the incident and wondering why she'd responded to him like… well, a woman on the prowl. It was done and she couldn't take any of it back. Now all she could do was try to face him as though nothing had ever happened.

After a hurried shower, she pulled on jeans, boots and a green hooded sweatshirt, quickly braided her hair into a single tail down her back, then swiped on sunscreen and scurried out of the bedroom.

When she arrived in the kitchen it was empty and the only sign that anyone had been there before her was a half pot of coffee still on the warmer.

Even though it was only seven-thirty, Hayley had obviously already left for school. There was no sight or sound of her anywhere. Last night Dallas hadn't asked the girl how she got to school or even where the school was located. If Boone drove her every day, he might be gone from the ranch for a while.

Not taking time to linger over breakfast, she found a banana from a bowl on the table and after gobbling the piece of fruit and washing it down with a half cup of the strong coffee, she grabbed her ranch jacket and headed out of the house.

As soon as she stepped onto the screened-in back porch, freezing north wind blasted her face. Immediately, she fished gloves and a sock cap from the patch pocket on her jacket and slipped them on. Once she was protected, she trotted down the steps with the intention of heading to the barns, but the sound of a vehicle at the front of the house caught her attention and she abruptly changed directions.

When she rounded the house, she was stunned to see a wrecker had already backed up to the rear of her truck and a small man dressed in heavy, dark blue coveralls was connecting the two vehicles with a wench. Boone was standing to one side, watching the whole process with a grim expression.

Dallas hurried over to him. "I see you've already called the wrecker," she said in a voice loud enough to be heard above the idling diesel engine of the tow truck.

"I didn't see any point in waiting. I figured you'd want it fixed as soon as possible."

He was right, Dallas thought. Still, it irked her that he'd taken on the task without bothering to ask her first. And though it was a ridiculous thought, something about seeing her only link to civilization being taken away left her feeling a bit desperate.

"I do want it repaired as quickly as possible," she replied. "But can't he try working on it here first? Before going to the trouble of pulling it off to Pioche? Maybe it's just a wire, or something simple like that."

"He's already tried," Boone said. "And I'm sorry, but he doesn't think it's a simple problem. He says the truck will have to be hooked up to a diagnostic machine and then he'll know more. But I can assure you that Marti knows his business and he's very trustworthy." Reaching for her elbow, he urged her toward the mechanic. "Come with me and I'll introduce you."

From the agile way Marti Alvarez had been scampering around and beneath her truck, Dallas was expecting him to be a much younger man. But one close look at his wrinkled face told her that he had to be several years beyond standard retirement age.

Once Boone had made a quick introduction and Dallas had given the mechanic a handshake, she asked the dreaded question. "How long to get it fixed?"

"Can't tell you that, miss, until I figure out what the problem actually is. If I'm guessing right and the fuel injector pump will have to be replaced, you're probably looking at two or three days. If a hole has been knocked in a piston, it'll take a lot longer."

Dallas gasped with shock. "Two or three days! Or longer! But I can't be here for that long!" She cast a horrified glance at Boone, then turned her gaze back on the mechanic. "Look, I'll pay you extra if you'll work on it today."

His smile indulgent, Marti swung his head back and forth. "I already plan to work on it today. I don't expect extra pay for that."

"Yes, but if you have customers ahead of me—" She broke off, knowing she sounded like a spoiled, privileged person trying to buy her way with money.

"Other customers aren't the problem, miss. Parts have to be ordered and shipped. Not to mention a day for tearing down and a day for putting everything back."

So she was well and truly stuck. The overwhelming thought made her want to wail with frustration. "Yes. I understand. And I'm sorry if I sounded ungrateful." She cast a furtive glance at Boone, then planted her focus back on the little mechanic. "Do you mind if I hitch a ride into town with you? I'll need a minute or two to gather up my things."

"Sure, I—"

Before the mechanic could get the rest of his words out, Boone stepped up to intervene. "Forget it, Marti, Ms. Donovan won't be going with you."

Stunned by Boone's interruption, she whirled on him. "What do you—"

Before she could finish, Boone caught her by the upper arm and pulled her a few steps away from Marti's ear-shot.

"What the hell are you thinking?" he demanded.

"Why the hell are you interrupting?" she shot back at him. "I don't have to tell you that I'm afoot! I have to get to town—"

"For what? You came to Nevada for horses," he pointed out. "In case you've forgotten, they're not in town. They're here."

Her mouth fell open. "What is this?" she asked furiously. "You've gone from kissing me to thinking you own me?"

A dull flush crept up his neck and jaws. "I'm trying to make sense here, that's all."

Throwing up her hands in a hopeless gesture, she said, "Then you should understand that I need transportation. I need to rent a vehicle."

"For what?"

Incredulous, Dallas stared at him. "To get back and forth from here to the hotel and—"

"What's the matter now?" he interjected. "The bed not comfortable enough? You were cold and needed more covers? Or you wanted room service?"

His light sarcasm caused her cheeks to blush red with anger, and her lips formed a thin line.

She wanted to shout at him that her sleepless night had nothing to do with the bed and everything to do with that damned kiss he'd planted on her. But she wasn't about to let him know that he'd affected her that deeply.

Blowing out a long breath, she clung to the last shreds of her composure. "I was perfectly comfortable. Thank you. But my food and lodging for this trip is not your responsibility. All I'm trying to do is get out of your hair."

To her surprise, humor flickered in his eyes. "I don't think feeding one little woman for a few days will break me. And believe me, if you get in my hair, I'll let you know about it."

Dallas had never been able to stay angry with anyone and as she looked at Boone she realized he was actually trying to help, even though he'd done it in a domineering way.

Allowing a faint smile to tilt her lips, she said, "I agree, it does make more sense for me to stay here, but I don't like the idea of taking advantage of your hospitality—that's all."

"If you feel that badly about it, just tack a few more dollars on the check you write for the horses. Besides, Hayley will be thrilled to have you here."

Hayley. Spending time with the girl last night had been more than enjoyable for Dallas. Though she couldn't understand or explain it, she'd felt an almost immediate bond with the child. The chance to be in her company a bit longer was enough to persuade Dallas to stay here on the ranch.

"All right, then. I'll tell Marti I don't need to hitch that ride after all."

Five minutes later, the tow truck and Dallas's broken vehicle pulled away from the house and headed south, across the dusty, open range of White River Ranch. As Dallas watched her only means of independence disappear from sight, Boone stood a few steps away watching her.

"I forgot to tell you last night that I have to drive Hayley to the school bus stop every morning. It's ten miles away, so I'm usually gone for thirty or forty minutes. Same goes in the evening to pick her up. Did you find something for breakfast while I was out?"

"Yes, thanks." Since he was unaware of exactly how late she'd slept, she wasn't going to admit that all she'd had time to eat was a banana. "Do you and Hayley have breakfast together before she has to leave for school?"

A wan smile crossed his face, and not for the first time, Dallas noticed that he'd not bothered to shave this morning. The dark brown stubble that covered his jaws, chin and upper lip made him look almost as wild and rangy as the horses he trained, and as she looked at him, she couldn't help wondering how it would feel to have that stubble rubbed against her cheek and breasts, to feel its roughness beneath her lips....

Embarrassed by the erotic thoughts going through her head, she looked beyond his shoulder at the gathering clouds and tried to forget that the two of them were well and truly alone.

"Hayley would rather sleep than eat at five-thirty when I do. She takes something with her and eats it on the way to the bus stop," he answered, then gestured in the direction of the barns. "Let's go have a look at the horses. I've already fed them so the kicking and maneuvering for special spots at the feed trough is already over with."

He took off in a long stride and, grateful for anything to break her train of thought, Dallas hurried after him. They were almost to the barns and corrals when the black-and-white shepherd dog joined them.

Boone introduced her as Queenie and Dallas quickly dropped to a squat so she could greet the dog on her level. Sensing that Dallas was a friend, Queenie gave her a big canine welcome by placing a paw on each of her shoulders and licking her cheek.

Laughing, Dallas said, "I think she likes me."

"Good thing. 'Cause she doesn't take well to strangers."

Dallas gave the dog's head an affectionate rub before

straightening to her full height. "You know a friend when you see one, don't you, girl?"

Queenie barked as though she understood every word Dallas had uttered, then followed close on her heels as they moved on to the corral full of horses.

Next to her, Boone shook his head with disbelief. "I should've warned you beforehand that Queenie has been known to snap at people she doesn't like. But I didn't want you to appear afraid."

"Gee, thanks," Dallas said dryly. "What were you planning on doing, letting her bite my hand off?"

He chuckled. "No. I had a feeling that you had a way with animals."

She cast him a droll look. "Maybe I do. But just be sure you don't neglect to warn me about an outlaw horse. I don't particularly want to be hospitalized with a broken bone while I'm waiting for my truck to be repaired."

He feigned an offended look. "The only outlaw I own is my personal horse. He's mean. But so am I. So that makes us a good pair."

Boone, mean? Domineering, perhaps, and a bit cynical, but not mean. Then again, one evening of light conversation, along with a very hot kiss, wasn't enough to show her every side of this Nevada rancher.

"Is that why you keep him?" she asked curiously. "Dad won't keep an outlaw on the place. He says you can feed a good horse for the same price you can feed a bad one."

"Sounds like your father is a wise man."

Dallas's chuckle was full of affection. "He's raised six kids. He's practical."

A faint semblance of a smile touched his face. "Well, Chester is a good working ranch horse. He just happens to have an attitude. But I've learned to deal with that."

Apparently dealing with Chester was easier than dealing with a wife with an attitude, Dallas thought. He'd made concessions for the horse, but not his wife? Or had the woman simply been impossible to deal with?

Forget it, she told herself. Forget what the man might have been like as a husband or what sort of husband he might be now.

But she couldn't forget. Not after that kiss he'd given her.

Pulling her gaze away from him, she turned it toward the corral and the small herd of horses. "I'm glad you have a bit of patience because I should warn you that I'm slow to make up my mind. It may take me a while to choose the mustangs I want to take back to New Mexico with me."

"Take all the time you want," he said. "I have all day. And from the looks of things, so do you."

His lazily spoken observation only served to remind Dallas that the two of them were miles and miles from another human being and, even if she wanted, she had no way of getting off this ranch or away from him. Unless he offered her a way.

Trying to ignore the nervous flutter in her stomach, she said, "Okay, I'll pick the ones that first catch my eye and then you can tell me about them."

"Fine. Let's get to work."

For the next two hours hour they walked among and around the thirty or so horses while Dallas studied each one for confirmation and attitude. Eventually, she chose six from the herd—a coal-black stallion, a sorrel filly with a blaze face, a little bay gelding that was hardly bigger than a pony, a brown mare with white socks, a shy chestnut filly and a buckskin gelding with a long, shaggy mane and forelock that covered his entire neck and most of his face.

After they haltered and tethered her choices to a hitching post in front of the barn, Dallas stepped back to give the animals another long, thoughtful consideration.

A few steps away, Boone said, "Considering that kids will eventually be riding them, I think you've made good choices. They're all gentle with no bad habits. But I insist that you handle and ride them yourself before you make a final decision. I want you to be completely satisfied."

She pulled her eyes away from the horses to look at him and even though he was standing three or four steps away, the impact of his gaze was still enough to shake her. "You say that like you're giving me a guarantee."

"I am," he said without hesitation. "If you get them back to your ranch and decide you don't like them—for any reason—just bring them back here to me and I'll refund your money."

The drive back would be bad enough, she thought, but seeing him again? Oh, no. This one time would be quite enough for her peace of mind.

She asked, "You do that for all of your buyers?"

One corner of his mouth lifted and without even realizing it, her breath caught in her throat and stayed there.

"Most. Not all."

She swallowed and forced herself to breathe. "Well, trust me, when I take on a responsibility it stays with me. I don't give it back or try to give it away just because something turns out to be more difficult than I first thought. As for the horses, I don't expect them to be perfect. Nothing or no one is."

"That's fair enough," he replied. "But just remember that my offer will always stand—even years from now."

Years? Dallas's gaze traveled beyond the quiet conviction on his face to the horses standing calmly at the hitching post. And it suddenly dawned on her that Boone wasn't going out of his way just to make sure she received fair dealings. This was more about him and the horses. He'd invested more than just his time and effort into the animals. His heart was involved.

The idea both touched and surprised her. He might view himself as mean as Chester, but his heart was most definitely soft.

"I'll remember," she murmured.

He cleared his throat, then said in a husky voice, "If you don't mind, we'll use my tack to saddle them up. It's right here in this barn and would save digging everything out of your trailer."

"Fine," she agreed.

Boone chose the stallion and led him into the barn and Dallas followed them into the dim interior of the metal structure. At the end of a wide alleyway, Boone dropped the lead rope and entered a door to his left. Dallas was impressed to see the horse didn't move an inch, even after he reappeared with a saddle and blanket and tossed it onto the animal's back.

Not one to just stand by and watch, Dallas quickly moved up on the right side of the horse and passed the leather cinch beneath its belly and up to Boone's waiting hand.

He was pulling the strap tight when the sound of a vehicle sounded just outside of the barn. Surprised by the unexpected noise, Dallas glanced over her shoulder to see a black, older model pickup truck barrel past the open doorway of the barn, then skid to a halt in front of a nearby shed.

"Were you expecting company?" she asked.

"That's Mick, my hired hand."

Boone had hardly gotten the words out of his mouth,

when a man appeared in the open entrance of the barn and started walking in their direction.

"Hey, Boone, what happened? Did you win the lottery or did the banker finally cave in and give you that loan? Man, when you decided to buy a new horse trailer, you decided to go whole hog, didn't you?"

"It's not mine, Mick."

"Not yours! Who—"

The remainder of the man's sentence stopped abruptly as he spotted Dallas stepping from behind the stallion and into the open.

"Oh. Oooh!" He moved forward, his appreciative gaze glued to Dallas. "Marti told me he'd come out here to collect a horse buyer's truck that had gone kaput. The old fox didn't mention a beautiful woman being here. I didn't know you had company, too, Boone."

"Dallas isn't company. She's the horse buyer." Boone curtly corrected the other man.

Mick didn't wait for Boone to make introductions; he quickly stepped closer and offered his hand to Dallas.

"Hello, I'm Mick Tanner. Boone's sidekick."

"Sidekick, hell," Boone muttered. "Don't pay any attention to him, Dallas. He's watched so many old Westerns that he's stuck in the 1940s and can't get out. Just look at those boots! A waste of good money if I ever seen it."

Dallas glanced down to see the man's jeans were stuffed into a pair of knee-high cowboy boots with flashy red-and-yellow inlays sewn in the shape of a thunderbird on the front of the shafts. Immediately she thought of Abe Cantrell back home. The old man would definitely smile if he could see Mick's choice of fancy footwear.

She smiled at the man with blue, blue eyes and a shock of sandy-blond hair covered by a gray cowboy hat. "It's nice to meet you, Mick. I'm Dallas Donovan—from New Mexico."

Mick gave her hand one last shake, then politely stepped back. "My pleasure," he said, then cut his eyes toward Boone. "Guess you can tell my boss doesn't have too much of a sense of humor."

"Well, you two just probably aren't amused by the same things," she said with as much diplomacy as she could.

Mick let out a generous laugh. "That's putting it mildly."

Boone glanced pointedly at the watch on his wrist. "Weren't you supposed to be here an hour ago?" he asked.

Mick chuckled again and Dallas could see that there was definitely a close understanding between the two men that only formed with longtime friendships.

"Yeah. But I had to spread hay for my own cattle this morning. And I met Marti on the way out here and we had to stop on the road and visit for a while. Remember his daughter? The older one with the black hair? Well, he says she's gotten divorced and is coming back to town. What does that tell ya?"

Boone let out a heavy sigh. "That you talk too much."

Mick shook his head. "Heck, Boone, it means that rich codger she married wasn't nearly as grand as she thought he was."

With a roll of his eyes, Boone turned back to the stallion and finished tucking the end of the cinch into the keeper. "Then she's probably coming back to town to get hooked up with you, Mick."

"That's exactly what I was thinking," he said with a grin, then turned a concerned look on Dallas. "So that was your truck Marti was towing. That's tough luck."

Dallas nodded. "Yes. Unfortunately, it's going to be out of service for a few days."

Mick's brows piqued with interest. "That's too bad. If you need a ride into town later today I'd be happy to give you a lift. Boone would rather chop off an arm than drive into town, so it would save him a trip."

"Forget it, Mick, Dallas doesn't need a lift."

Her mouth fell open as she whipped her head around to stare at Boone. Since when had he become her boss, she wanted to ask. From the moment she'd arrived here on the ranch he'd been trying to tell her what she should and shouldn't do. And if it weren't for Mick's presence, she'd promptly inform Mr. Boone Barnett that she didn't belong to him or any man. But he wasn't even bothering to look her way. Instead, he was bridling the black stallion as though the matter was already settled. And maybe it was, but that didn't give him the right to speak for her as though she was mute.

Seeing her dagger-filled gaze was lost on Boone, she turned a smile on Mick. "Thank you for the offer," she told the other man. "It was thoughtful of you, but I'll be staying here on the ranch until my truck is ready to drive again."

Surprise swept across Mick's face, then as he looked in Boone's direction, his initial shock was swiftly replaced by somber concern.

"Oh. Well, that's…good." He lifted the gray hat from his head and with his attention directed at the ground, he raked an awkward hand through his hair, then slapped the Stetson back on. "Well, I'm going to drive the old truck out to the windmill in the north pasture," he said for Boone's benefit. "I'll take the tools with me. Just in case it stopped working again."

"Fine. I'll see you later," Boone replied.

The other man quickly left the barn and Dallas moved back to the head of the horse. By now Boone had the bits and bridle in place and was adjusting the throat latch.

"Your friend seemed upset about something," she ventured to say. "And I think it concerns me staying here on the ranch. I don't get it."

"Forget about Mick," he said curtly. "He needs to mind his own business."

"But you two must be good friends. I don't—"

Boone moved around the horse's head to where she was standing. "Look, Dallas, Mick thinks every pretty girl within a two-hundred-mile radius is his for the taking. He's just miffed because you won't be riding into town with him, that's all."

Dallas believed there was much more to the man's abrupt change in mood than the explanation Boone had given her, but she wasn't going to push the issue. After all, her host could handle his own affairs, especially if he stayed out of hers.

"Well, are all the girls his for the taking?" she asked with an impish grin.

He grimaced. "I'll put it this way, he's gone through his share of them. And that's—" He stopped abruptly and when Dallas continued to wait for him to finish, he said gruffly, "Let's not talk about Mick. Especially behind his back."

Dallas could appreciate the man's loyalty to his friend and she especially didn't want to come off looking like a gossiper, so she smiled in agreement.

"Fine with me. Is the stallion ready to ride?"

"Yes. I'll lead him outside and you can mount up there."

Taking up the reins, Boone led the horse out of the barn while Dallas followed close behind.

By now the sun was being covered by a blanket of thin winter clouds. As she paused to tighten the scarf around her neck, she took a moment to scan the distant horizon. The terrain surrounding the ranch and barns was completely open, with nothing to see except a few distant hills and a handful of cattle. Since she was used to mountains covered with green forests and valley meadows thick with lush grass, the dry desolation of the land amazed her.

"What's wrong?"

Boone's question pulled her head around to see that he was standing beside the horse, clearly waiting for her to finish her daydreaming.

Stepping closer, she shook her head. "Sorry. I was just looking at your land. It's so different from what I'm used to. Is there anything out there? I mean, other than those distant hills and the far-off mountains? I can't see anything but desert floor."

Faint amusement touched the corners of his mouth and Dallas's gaze zeroed in on the hard lips that had rocked over hers in a kiss that she still couldn't push from her mind.

"You mean is there life out there? Yeah. A thousand head of Angus cattle and half that many more cross-breeds. Not to mention a band of wild mustangs that appear now and then, wild burros and all sorts of smaller creatures, like antelope, deer, coyotes, jackrabbits and even mountain lions. And in the spring migrating birds use this area to rest before they move on north."

A pink blush settled across her cheeks. "I feel like a fool for being so ignorant. To me it just looks…desolate. Like nothing could survive out there."

"That's why the wildlife does survive out there, because nothing is out there to disturb it. Like towns and land developers."

She studied him thoughtfully. "I think you're a bit like all that wildlife you just mentioned. You'd rather not have people around you...messing up things and causing you problems."

With a negligent shrug, he turned to the stallion and rechecked the tightness of the saddle cinch. "So you've decided I'm a loner. Is that what you're saying?"

"I guess I am."

"And you disapprove."

Even though he'd made a statement rather than a question, she answered just the same. "I didn't say that."

With his forearm resting against the saddle, he turned slightly toward her and Dallas was suddenly hit hard by the rough, sexy image he projected in his worn jeans, rugged wool jacket and battered black cowboy hat. Mick might be attractive in a smooth, blue-eyed way. But Boone was dark and smoldering and just mysterious enough to keep her looking and wondering.

He said, "You were thinking it."

"Well, I'm basically an outdoor gal, but I also like people. Young and old. The more I have around me, the more I like it. And I like going to town and enjoying all the fun things it has to offer. Maybe that's just the woman in me. Or maybe it has something to do with the fact that the Diamond D has always been full of people. We employ at least a hundred people and there are always horse racing folks and other friends hanging around to add to the mix. I've never been around this much—" she gestured out toward the open, sweeping land "—solitude before. I'd have to have a powerful reason to live out here."

His face was emotionless as he looked at her. "And

I'd have to have a powerful reason not to," he said, then made a forward gesture with his thumb. "C'mon and I'll give you a leg up."

Dallas tried not to appear wary as she stepped closer to him and the horse, but he must have read her thoughts, or at least part of them.

"Don't worry," he said gruffly. "I'm not going to grab you and kiss you again."

She resisted the urge to swallow. "What makes you think I'm worried?"

The cynical slant of his lips belied the faint gleam of amusement in his eyes. "Probably the way you're sidling up to me like I'm a hungry coyote."

"Nothing wrong with a coyote," she quipped. "At least he mates for life."

His nostrils flared. "Like I said before, I don't plan on kissing you again."

For some reason his cocky promise raked over every womanly particle inside of Dallas and before she realized what she was doing, she'd moved close enough to stick her face right in front of his. "I think you're the one who's worried, Boone."

She watched his gaze dropped to her lips and anticipation shivered right through her.

"Me?" he asked softly. "What do I have to be worried about?"

"That you kissed me—and you liked it."

Chapter Five

Dallas didn't know what had possessed her to throw such a taunt at Boone. He wasn't the sort of man who would take a dare lightly, even from a woman.

And he didn't.

The next thing Dallas knew she was crushed tightly against him and her mouth was completely captured beneath his lips.

In spite of the cold wind whipping through the barnyard and slapping at the side of her face, Dallas was instantly suffused with heat from the top of her head right down to the soles of her feet. The taste of his lips was a dark, mysterious promise that made her want more and more.

Instinctively, her arms crept up and around his neck and her mouth opened even wider to accept the gentle prod of his tongue. At the same time, his hands slipped beneath the hem of her jacket and latched onto the sides of her waist. When he pulled her hips forward to press against his, she groaned deep in her throat and tightened her fingers against the back of his neck.

Drawn deeper and deeper into a swirl of sweet sensations, Dallas was stunned when his mouth suddenly ripped from hers and he shoved an arm's length of distance between them. "Better be careful, Ms. Donovan, this coyote might turn into a wolf," he warned softly. "Or is that what you're aiming for—to knock me off balance?"

Struggling to pull herself from the dreamy fog of his kiss, she sucked in a deep breath and hoped the cold wind would fade the hot color in her cheeks.

"I'm not the one who started this," she said in a low, strained voice.

"Maybe not. But you can damned well be sure that *I'm* going to be the one who ends it."

This time Dallas wasn't going to argue, nor was she about to fling another taunt at him. For the next few days she had to live under the same roof with this man and that didn't include falling into bed with him.

Just remember, honey, if you play with fire, you're likely to get burned.

Her grandmother Kate's sage advice had often been repeated to Dallas and her two sisters as they'd gone through their teenaged dating years. And though that time in her life was long past, the hackneyed warning aptly fit her present situation. Boone Barnett was definitely too much fire for Dallas to handle.

Her nostrils flaring with disgust that was aimed at herself and him, she turned toward the stallion and snatched up the bridle reins. "You won't have to. It's ended," she said flatly. "Let's get on with the horses. After all, that's why I'm here."

She jammed the toe of her boot in the stirrup and started to swing herself onto the horse's back, but before she could lift her other foot off the ground, Boone's hands wrapped around her waist and lifted her up and into the saddle.

The innocuous touch shouldn't have affected her. Especially when back on the Diamond D there were plenty of ranch hands around who were always more than eager to give her a leg up. She never gave their physical assistance a second thought. But it was different with Boone. Oh, so different.

"Thanks," she said stiffly as she settled herself in the saddle seat.

With his hand resting alarmingly close to her thigh, he glanced up at her. "He's not wearing a bit, just a hackamore."

She focused her gaze on the long black mane lying thickly on the left side of the horse's neck. It was certainly a safer sight than Boone's stony face, she thought. "I had already noticed that."

He added, "You don't need to use a heavy hand to get him to respond."

She wasn't a greenhorn, she wanted to scream at him. She'd grown up in the saddle and was considered by most to be an excellent horsewoman. But just as quickly she reminded herself that this man didn't know that about her. He was only trying to protect his horse.

"Don't worry," she said in a gentler tone, "I'll get the feel of him."

She pressed her heels into the horse's sides and Boone immediately stepped back as she rode away from him.

What in hell was he thinking? He mentally yelled the question at himself as he watched Dallas ease the stallion into a faster walk. More importantly what was *she* thinking? About him and that kiss he planted on her last night? And now—damn it, he might as well have hung a sign around his neck saying, *I want to kiss you, touch you all over, carry you to my bed and make love to you for hours.*

Muttering a curse to himself, Boone swiped a hand over his face, then pressed his thumb and forefinger against his closed eyes.

This wasn't like him. Boone knew it. And so did Mick. He'd not missed the look of shock on his friend's face when Dallas had explained to him that she'd be staying on the ranch for the next few days. For the past year or so Boone hadn't even bothered to date. And he'd sure as heck never had female guests in his house. He didn't want any woman *that* close to him. Nor did he want one getting close to Hayley. Joan had pushed the both of them through a wringer and left them to hang in the desert wind. He and his daughter didn't need the risk of being hurt like that again.

So why had he insisted on Dallas staying on the ranch? Now he couldn't keep his hands off her. And she wasn't helping matters with the way she'd melted against him. She'd kissed him as though she'd really wanted to kiss him, as though he was somebody special.

Special hell, he silently grunted. She was clearly a ranching heiress. She could have her pick of men and it sure wouldn't include a horse trainer and cattle rancher who had to work from sunup to sundown just to scratch out a meager living. No. Kisses or not, he had to quit making a fool of himself.

Heaving out a sigh, he dropped his hand and gazed across the open ranch yard to see that Dallas was already cantering the stallion in a figure-eight pattern. The sight had him momentarily forgetting about the hot kiss they'd just exchanged. He was instantly awed by the perfect way she sat in the saddle and the subtle cues her hands and legs gave instructing the horse. She definitely knew what she was doing and then some.

For the next few minutes, she put the horse through a series of roll-backs, turns and stops. His hands jammed in the pockets of his jacket, Boone stood where he was and watched until she finally rode over to him and dismounted with a lithe jump.

"He's fabulous, Boone! He practically knew what I wanted from him before I ever asked." Her lips spread into a wide smile. "You've done a wonderful job with him. Really wonderful!"

Boone tried to remain indifferent to her compliment, but he couldn't deny the warm rush of feelings pouring through him. To have an excellent horsewoman praise his efforts was one thing, but she was also beautiful and classy, and could have her pick of horses and trainers.

"Thanks. I've got ninety days of training in him."

Her eyes widened with amazement. "That's all? Oh, wow! You *are* good."

Before he even realized it, Boone was chuckling at her remark. "Dallas, didn't your father ever tell you that you should keep your thoughts to yourself when you're dealing for horses?"

She laughed outright and the sound pleased him far more than it should have. She had a sweet, rich laugh that danced over his senses like sunshine sparkling on water.

"I'd make a terrible poker player. When I like something I don't hide my feelings. Besides, I'm not one to bargain. If I believe a price is fair, then I buy. If not, I simply say thanks and be on my way."

When I like something I don't hide my feelings. She certainly hadn't tried to hide them when he'd been kiss-

ing her, Boone thought. Just the memory of her lips open-
ing beneath his, her arms slipping around his neck, was
enough to curl his toes. But that was over. He had to
make sure it was over.

"I promise the price will be fair," he said.

She turned back to the horse and stroked a hand
against his neck. "Does he have a name?"

"No. I don't name the ones I train to sell. It makes it
easier whenever I have to let them go." Dear God, she
was probably thinking he was as soft as cornmeal mush.
But he wasn't going to pretend that he didn't get attached
to the mustangs. Aside from his daughter, they were his
whole life. He spent hours and hours each day in their
company. How could he not love them?

"Well, I think I'll call him Midnight. Not too imagi-
native. But he's dark and peaceful, like the middle of a
quiet night."

He watched her fingers continue to stroke slowly and
smoothly down the horse's shoulder. "Does that mean
you want him?"

Twisting her head around, she looked at him with surprise. "Of course!"

"But I haven't quoted a price to you yet."

A slow grin spread across her lips and Boone felt the
heat that was already simmering low in his belly threaten
to leap into a flame.

"You said you'd be fair and I trust you to keep your
word."

Something in her voice said she was talking about
more than the price of a horse and the idea jolted him.
Joan had once trusted him with her very happiness and
he'd let her down. Before Dallas left the ranch, he figured he'd probably let her down, too.

"All right." He reached for the stallion's reins. "Let's

take your Midnight back to the barn and saddle up another one."

"Oh, let's do the brown mare next," she said as they quickly strode toward the group of tethered horses. "I've already decided that she's Princess."

Her excitement was contagious and Boone couldn't stop himself from smiling. "You can already tell that title fits her, can you?"

She laughed. "The moment I looked in her eyes."

For the first time Boone could remember, the morning passed too quickly. When Mick drove back into the ranch yard it was nearly noon and Dallas had already gone into the house to find something for lunch. He'd just finished hanging a saddle in the tack room and was on his way out of the barn when his friend met him in the open doorway.

"Was the windmill working?" Boone asked before the other man had a chance to speak.

"No. But there was plenty of water left in the tank. I've been trying to fix the thing for the past two hours. It's going right now. But I wouldn't hold my breath."

Boone grimaced. "We're going to have to replace the old thing. It's causing us more time and trouble than it's worth. And I don't want that tank going dry."

"No. It's probably a good two-mile trip to the other one," Mick said, then glanced curiously around Boone's shoulder and into the dim cavern of the barn. "Ms. Donovan gone in the house?"

"She got hungry for lunch," Boone explained. "I was just about to join her. You want to eat with us?"

Mick cast him a droll glance. "Three makes one too many. I've got a sandwich in the truck anyway. I'm gonna wolf it down, then saddle up and check that fence line down by the riverbed."

Boone pushed the brim of his hat slightly off his brow as he studied his longtime friend. He should ignore Mick's comment about one too many, but he couldn't let it slide. Mick had been his friend for thirty-four years, ever since they'd walked in Miss Grayson's kindergarten class the very first day. The two had been through thick and thin together and he was the closest thing to a brother Boone would ever have.

"There's no need for you to choke down your sandwich out here. Dallas and I don't need the kind of privacy you're thinking about. For Pete's sake, I've just met the woman."

Mick's expression was uncharacteristically serious as he looked at Boone. "Yeah. And from the way things look you must have gotten acquainted real quick."

"What does that mean?"

Mick shot him a look of disbelief. "You have to ask? Since when has a woman spent the night in your house—other than your mother when she was still living?"

Boone shook his head. "None. But you're reading way too much in this, Mick. The woman's truck broke down. Where else was she going to stay?"

"How about a hotel in town? That's the logical place."

That's what Dallas had said, too. But Boone had talked her out of it. And right now he didn't want to dig too deeply into his reasons. Common, logical sense was enough of a motive for now.

He glanced away from Mick and over to the small dusty lot holding the six horses Dallas had chosen to take back to New Mexico with her. He was going to miss the four-legged critters. And he was going to miss her. That much he already knew. Damn it.

He turned his gaze back on his friend. "Mick, the woman drove nearly a thousand miles to buy horses from me, the least I can do is offer her a bit of hospitality. Especially when she's virtually stranded."

"You like her, don't you?"

The two men rarely discussed women. What was the point? Mick had as many as he wanted and Boone wanted none. There was nothing for them to talk about.

"You're being ridiculous, Mick."

"Am I?"

Boone mouthed a curse word under his breath. "What if I said I did like the woman? What if I said I was happy about her hanging around for a few days? So what? It's my business."

The other man's face paled just a fraction and Boone realized he'd not only shocked him, but he'd also angered him.

"Yeah, it's your business. What the hell am I worried about it for anyway?" Mick growled back at him.

"That's right! Why are you worried? Afraid this is one you won't get?"

His jaw rock-hard, Mick glared at him. "That was uncalled for."

"This whole conversation is uncalled for," Boone snarled back at him, then turned in the direction of the house. "I'm going in for lunch. You do what you want to do."

As Boone started striding away, Mick called out, "I will."

"Fine," Boone grumbled and continued walking.

Later that evening, after Dallas had spent most of the afternoon watching Boone work with the mustangs he was currently training, they returned to the house to find that Marti had left a message for Dallas on the answering machine. Her truck needed a new injector pump and the part would have to be ordered, he'd said. And barring no major problems, the truck would probably be ready to drive in three days.

Three days! By then it would be the twenty-third of December. To get home for Christmas Eve she'd have to drive straight through, and she wasn't sure she was up to sitting behind the wheel of a truck for seventeen or more hours.

Trying not to display her disappointment, Dallas sank onto the end of the couch. "Well, I guess I'd better let my family know what's going on. They were expecting me to start back home today."

Boone gestured to the phone that was sitting on a table to the right of her. "Go ahead and make the call. I've got to drive to the school bus stop to pick up Hayley. I'll be gone for a half hour, at least."

"Thanks," she said, then asked, "Is there anything I can do to help out while you're gone?"

His brows lifted. "Do you know how to cook?"

She chuckled. "Not really. But I can try." For lunch she'd dumped a can of tuna on a plate, added a few saltine crackers and a pickle and called it a meal. As for Boone, it was his food and his kitchen and he'd obviously been doing for himself for years, so she'd let him deal with fixing his own lunch.

His mouth slanted to a wry smile. "Don't worry about it. I'll fix something later."

Dallas watched him leave the room, while thinking *later* meant after he got back with Hayley and after he fed and watered several corrals full of horses. Even if she wasn't the best of cooks, she had to find some way to help, she thought. It was the least she could do to compensate for her room and board.

Sighing, she reached for the phone and dialed her brother's cell number. Her first attempt to reach him failed, so she tried again, hoping the strange number wouldn't put him off.

Thankfully he answered the second time she rang and she sighed with relief when she heard her brother's voice come over the phone.

"Liam, it's me, Dallas."

"Dallas! Where in the world are you? That wasn't your number on my caller ID."

"My cell won't work where I am right now," she explained.

"And where is that?"

"I'm still on the White River Ranch."

"Still? I thought you were going to be loaded and leaving early this morning. Is anything wrong?"

Dallas rubbed the heel of her palm nervously against the denim fabric covering her thigh. "Well...actually, there is. But don't worry. I've got it all under control."

There was a long pause and then Liam's skeptical voice sounded in her ear. "You've wrecked my truck, or the trailer—or both! Are you all right, Dallas? If you're hurt—"

Just the thought of anyone in the family being in a highway collision was enough to send Liam into a panic. He'd lost his wife, unborn child and mother-in-law all in one fatal moment when their car had crashed on a foggy mountain roadway. "I'm sorry, Liam, I should have told you right off that I'm perfectly okay."

He let out a long breath of relief. "Good. I can deal with any other problem. Even if you have crunched up my new truck," he added with a dose of affectionate teasing.

"Well, the problem is the truck," Dallas admitted. "But no—I didn't wreck it. Something went haywire with it and a wrecker had to haul it from the ranch back into the closest town. Now the mechanic tells me it will be three days before he can have it repaired."

"Something went haywire!" he exclaimed with disbelief. "It's only been driven a few thousand miles."

"An injector pump has to be replaced—or I think that's what the mechanic called it. Anyway, the part has to be ordered and you know how it is to get anything repaired." Reaching into the pocket of her jeans, she pulled out Marti's business card. "I can give you the mechanic's number if you'd like to talk to him."

"No. That's okay. I trust you to take care of it. Just as long as you made sure that he's a reputable repairman."

"Boone says he's the best. And frankly, this place is in the middle of nowhere, Liam. There aren't exactly a lot of choices around here in the way of auto repairs or anything else for that matter."

He didn't immediately reply and Dallas figured her brother was about to explode into a rant. At one time Liam had been a gentle, loving man who rarely raised his voice, but losing his young family along with the eighteen-hour days he put in as the Diamond D's horse trainer had changed him. She loved him deeply, but from day to day it was anyone's guess as to the mood they'd find him in.

"This Boone—is he the man you're buying the horses from?"

"That's right."

"Is he trustworthy?"

Dallas gripped the phone. If necessary, she'd trust

Boone with her life. Funny how short of time it had taken for her to come to that conclusion about him. "Yes," she answered. "And he's lived here all his life, so he's well acquainted with the mechanic."

"I see. Then let's not worry about the truck. You might as well hop on a plane and come home. After Christmas we'll fly back up there and collect the truck, trailer and horses."

"But Liam—"

"You don't want to miss Christmas with your family, do you?"

Her brother's question prompted her to look around the Barnett's family room. There was not one sign of the oncoming holiday. Not even one poinsettia leaf, one twinkling light or even a simple candle. From the looks of things, Boone and Hayley didn't celebrate Christmas. The notion was a hard one for Dallas to swallow. During the Christmas season, the Diamond D was always one bustling party.

"No. But hopping on a plane is not that simple, Liam. I told you this place is in the middle of nowhere. Boone tells me it's a hundred miles or more to the nearest airport and that's over in Utah." And she wasn't about to ask him to drive her such a lengthy distance. Even if she offered to pay Boone handsomely to make the trip, she knew his time meant far more to him than money. Besides, he had a daughter to deal with and she was much too young to leave on her own. "But everything will work out okay, Liam. If the truck is ready by the twenty-third, I can make it home for Christmas."

"And what will you do in the meantime?"

Dallas hesitated, but only for a moment. "I'm staying here on the ranch with the Barnett family."

"You're okay with that?"

The memory of Boone's kisses was suddenly all she could think of and she had to clear her voice before she could answer in a normal tone. "Sure. It's beautiful out here. And the family is nice. I'm actually enjoying it. So don't worry. I'll be home in a few days."

"If you're sure."

"I am," she replied. They talked a few more minutes about things going on at the ranch, then she wound up the conversation by giving Boone's landline number to her brother and advising him to leave a message if no one answered.

As she hung up the phone, the sensation that she was cutting all ties with her home and family hit her hard. And she quickly tried to counter it by telling herself how silly she was being. After all, she'd been away from home on numerous occasions before and even with this truck breakdown she wasn't going to be gone very long this time. But it was nearly Christmas and just the thought of not being on the ranch, celebrating with her family and friends, was enough to put her in a wistful mood.

Restlessly, she left the family room and walked out to the kitchen and stared out the single window situated over the sink. The sun was sinking low on the western horizon, bathing the flat sweep of land in streaks of pale yellow and purple. Slightly to the north, bald rolling hills rose up from the desert basin, then even farther in the distance there was a line of jagged mountains that appeared to be capped with snow.

When she'd told Liam that the White River Ranch was beautiful, she'd meant it. There was a majestic sort of awe to this land of Boone's. Yet admitting such a thing, even to herself, had been a surprise. She'd always believed no place could compare to the Hondo Valley, where the Diamond D sat nestled in the foothills of the Sierra Blanca

Range and Capitan Mountains. The Rio Hondo cut a path through the valley, where tall, cool shade trees followed its path. During the summer, farmers tended rows and rows of fruit trees and along the twisting highway, stands would appear to sell the sweet, succulent produce. Her grandmother Kate would always buy apple cider and in the winter, Opal, the ranch's cook, would spice it with cloves and heat it for a holiday drink.

Sighing wistfully, Dallas turned away from the window and the memories that were tugging on her emotions. Now wasn't the time to stand around pining for home. Right now she had to make the best of the situation and show Boone that she wasn't a helpless, ungrateful guest.

A half hour later, she was standing at the cookstove, stirring a skillet of hamburger hash, when the back door opened and Hayley came rushing in with a burst of cold wind. Dallas looked over her shoulder just in time to see Boone stepping through the doorway and as her gaze collided with his something yanked on her heart.

"Dad, look! Dallas is fixing dinner! And it smells so good!" the girl exclaimed.

While she hurriedly tossed her books onto the rolltop desk, Boone took off his jacket and hung it on a peg near the door.

"I see," he replied, then sauntered over to where Dallas stood with a wooden spoon in her hand. "You didn't have to do this, you know."

She looked at him and was amazed at how familiar his face had already become to her. Already she'd memorized the faint lines fanning from the corners of his brown eyes, the slight dent in his chin, the chiseled cheekbones and hard curve of his lower lip.

"I know. But I wanted to. Besides, it's not much. And

once you taste it, you might want to run to the wastebasket and spit it out."

"I don't believe that, Dallas!" Hayley said as she joined the two adults. "I'll bet it tastes as good as it smells. How long 'til it's done?"

"Five minutes," Dallas said with a smile for the girl. "How's that for timing?"

"Gee, that's great!" Her gaze switched over to her father. "Can you believe it, Dad, I don't have to do anything except sit down and eat."

He leveled a pointed look at his daughter. "Oh, yes, you do. First you've got to go wash up and after supper, you're going to have the whole job of cleaning up."

"Okay," she said with a negligible shrug. "Whatever you say, Dad."

She whirled on one toe and scurried from the room like a ballerina exiting the stage.

"She seems happy enough," Dallas commented as she watched Hayley disappear through a doorway on the opposite side of the room. "Has school let out for the holidays?"

"Yes, as of today, she'll be out until the Monday after New Year's." He looked past her shoulder to the bubbling meat mixture on the stove. "If that stuff will be ready in five minutes, I suppose I'll have to wait until after dinner to feed the horses."

"It can be reheated if you'd rather do your chores now. But if you'll wait until after we eat, I'll be glad to help you with the feeding."

"No! That's my job," he said quickly.

She arched a brow at him, then turned and switched off the flame from beneath the skillet. "Feeding horses is not a job to me. It's a joy. Don't deprive me."

"Dallas, helping out in the kitchen is one thing, but—"

Before he could say more, she twisted her head around to face him. "What do you want me to do, Boone? Go hide in my bedroom and not come out until it's time for me to go back to New Mexico?"

"No. But—"

"You can tell by looking at me that I'm not too delicate to lift a feed bucket," she interrupted. "And if you're worried about being alone in the dark with me, forget it. I promise not to get too close or try to seduce you."

A deep blush crawled up his throat and onto his jaws. "Damn it, Dallas, I'm trying to be a gentleman."

A faint smile curved her lips. "And I'm promising to be a lady. So the way I see it everything is settled nicely."

He frowned with frustration. "I don't need your help."

"No, but I'm giving it to you anyway," she countered. "And while I am you might discover it doesn't hurt to share things with someone, even work."

And even a kiss, Dallas wanted to add, but out of respect for his wishes, she kept the last thought to herself. He was clearly trying to keep a cool distance from her. And though that idea should have been reassuring, it wasn't. It stung. Deeply.

"I have Mick. And Hayley," he said in a low, clipped voice.

Her gaze dropped from his eyes to his lips. "Are they enough?" she asked softly.

A muscle twitched in his cheek. "They have to be."

The solemn conviction in his voice was so stark and lonely that tears were suddenly burning the inside of Dallas's throat. Dear God, what was happening to her? Keeping her hands off this man for the next three days was not going to be easy. But that was no longer her main worry. Now she had to find a way to stop herself from falling in love with him.

Chapter Six

Later that night, Boone sat with his head resting against the back of the stuffed armchair and his long legs stretched out in front of him. Except for two narrow slits, his eyes appeared to be closed, but he was having no problem seeing his daughter and Dallas as they sat several feet away from him on the couch.

At the moment, Hayley was doing most of the talking and punctuating every other word with a hand gesture. He'd never seen his daughter so animated before and though it was nice to see her clearly enjoying herself, he was worried.

Even though she often tried to play the tough girl with him, he knew there was an overly sensitive side to Hayley, and no one had to tell him that Joan was the cause of it. While his daughter had been only a very young child, Boone had tried to dodge her innocent questions as to why she didn't have a mommy like the rest of her friends. But as Hayley had grown old enough to understood, there'd been no way of getting around the issue and he'd had to be as honest as he could be. Joan simply hadn't been capable of being a nourishing mother to a child. Yet that didn't make up for the brutal fact that her mother refused to take any interest in her daughter's life.

Four days wasn't a long time, his thoughts continued. But it was long enough for Hayley to build a bond with Dallas. Hell, he was a grown man who knew better than to let his feelings get wrapped up in a person who would only be in his life for a very brief time. Yet she was slowly drawing him to her, even though he was fighting to keep his heels firmly stuck in the ground. What would it do to Hayley when the woman left? What would it do to him?

Today, as Dallas had worked beside him with the horses, it had given Boone a glimpse of how it might be to have a woman by his side, one who understood and appreciated his lifestyle. Joan had never been an outdoor person. In fact, she'd been too timid to even pet a horse, much less ride one. Cows had horrified her and dogs had disgusted her. Before they'd divorced, she'd described living on the ranch as being locked away in solitary confinement.

Looking back on it now, he wondered how or why they'd ever married. And looking forward he realized he couldn't make the mistake of confusing compatibility for love.

A few feet away on the couch, Dallas was completely aware of Boone's presence, yet she was making it a point to catch every word that Hayley uttered. The girl had opened the floodgates and so far showed no sign in shutting them.

"Do you like music, Dallas?" she asked as she absently twirled a strand of hair around one finger.

"Sure. I like all kinds of music. Why? Do you have a new CD you'd like for me to listen to?"

Hayley's shoulders scrunched upward in a bashful gesture. "Not really. I was wondering…well, if you'd like to hear me sing?"

Totally surprised, Dallas turned slightly toward the girl. "You sing?"

Hayley's cheeks turned bright pink. "Well, I'm not great at it or anything. But I take choir in school and tomorrow night I'm going to be in the Christmas play at our church and I play the part of a singing angel. Would you like to come?"

Just when Dallas had practically come to the conclusion that Boone and his daughter must practice some sort of religion that didn't involve celebrating Christmas, Hayley came out with this pleasant surprise.

"Oh, I'd love to attend," she assured the girl, then after a quick, guarded glance at Boone, she lowered her voice and added, "I've been wondering why you don't have any decorations around the house. Do you ever have a tree or anything like that for Christmas?"

Sighing, Hayley's expression turned glum. "Not since my grandma Elsa died. We used to have a tree then. But that was a long time ago—when I was seven."

To say that Dallas was shocked and disgusted was putting it mildly. "And you've not decorated for Christmas since then?"

Hayley shook her head. "Dad says since it's just me and him that there's not much point."

Dallas's lips pressed to a thin line as she looked directly over at Boone. "Well, I think it's high time we did something about that," she said to Hayley. "We'll drive—"

Her words came to an abrupt halt as it suddenly dawned on her that she couldn't drive anywhere. As far as transportation went, she was at Boone's mercy.

"I was about to say we'll drive into town and buy decorations," Dallas continued. "But seeing that my truck is on the blink, I can't do that."

Excitement was suddenly dancing in Hayley's eyes. "We have some old decorations in the attic, Dallas. They'd be better than nothing! Do you think we could get them down? Maybe we can talk Dad into getting a tree!"

"Would you like that?" Dallas asked gently.

"Ooooh, would I! We could have a real Christmas then!"

A real Christmas. Dallas's heart was suddenly aching as she studied Hayley's sweet little face. The child had been missing out on so much. And why? she wondered. Just because Boone wanted to hide from life didn't mean that his daughter wanted to, also.

Determined now, Dallas rose to her feet and reached for Hayley's hand. "C'mon. Show me where we can find these decorations."

"Yippee!" Hayley blurted as she jumped to her feet.

The commotion caused Boone to open his eyes and look at the two of them. "What's going on?" he asked Hayley.

Bouncing on her toes, she turned to her father. "Me and Dallas are going to get the Christmas decorations from the attic. She thinks we need a tree and so do I!"

His gaze settling on Dallas, he scooted to the edge of the chair. "Oh, she does, does she?"

Not waiting for Hayley to answer, Dallas spoke up.

"That's right. It would make the place more festive. Besides, where will Santa leave the presents if there isn't a tree?"

Hayley rolled her eyes. "Santa doesn't bring gifts. Dad just gives me money."

Dallas leveled a disapproving glare at him. "Is that right? You only give your daughter money?"

His eyes widened as though he couldn't believe Dallas had the audacity to question him about such personal things.

"She likes it," he said curtly. "Is that a crime or something?"

Dallas blew out a long breath. "It's a crime for you to be so indifferent. You—" Realizing that Hayley was standing at her side and taking in everything being said, Dallas stopped the sermon she would have liked to preach to the man. "Well, it's your business, not mine."

"I'm glad you realize that."

"What about the tree, Dad? Can we get one?"

Boone rose to his feet. "Hayley, it's dark outside."

The girl groaned with frustration. "They have lights in town."

Grimacing, Boone darted a look-what-you've-started glance at Dallas before he turned his full attention to Hayley. "We're not about to drive into town at this hour, especially since we have to make the drive tomorrow evening. If you want a tree that much, we'll go cut one here on the ranch."

The incredulous look on Hayley's face told Dallas that his concession was obviously a big deal that didn't happen often.

"Oh, Dad, really? Tomorrow?" Not waiting for him to answer, Hayley flung herself forward and wrapped her father in a tight hug. "Thank you! Thank you! This is going to be the best Christmas we've ever had!"

Whatever he might think of Dallas and her interference, he was clearly touched by his daughter's display of affection. He hugged her close, then after stroking a hand over her hair, he set her from him and looked at Dallas.

"Okay," he said. "If you two are so set on this, let's see if we have any luck finding those decorations."

The next morning Boone was sitting at the kitchen table nursing a cup of coffee and staring out the window at a black sky when Dallas walked through the open doorway.

She was still dressed in pajamas and a robe and her thick red hair was a tumble of waves upon her shoulders. It was only a quarter past five, but she didn't appear to be a bit groggy as she looked at him and smiled.

"Good morning," she greeted.

"Good morning."

She walked straight to the coffeepot. After she'd poured herself a mug and added cream, she joined him at the table.

Even before she took a seat Boone felt his pulse quicken, his senses go on high alert. She was definitely a beautiful ray of sunshine on a cold winter morning.

"There wasn't any need for you to get up so early," he said.

"I'm usually up earlier than this," she explained.

"Is that necessary? I mean, you surely have ranch hands to deal with things?"

"Oh, yes. I have help. But I've always been full of energy and I love what I do, so I'm always eager for the day to get started."

Sipping his coffee he tried to imagine her home and family. "Are your sisters anything like you?"

As she contemplated his question, her eyes softened with affection. "Somewhat. We're all energetic and outgoing. But my sisters are petite and soft and a lot brainier than me. I'm the physical one of us. I take after my grandmother Kate. She's eighty-four and still rides a horse nearly every day."

If the plane crash hadn't taken her, his grandmother would have been eighty now. How Boone wished she was still here to guide him when he felt lost, scold him when he made mistakes, love him when he was lonely.

"You're very lucky."

Something like guilt crossed her face and then her gaze dropped to the tabletop.

"I think I should apologize to you," she said.

"Why? You break something in your room?"

She smiled wanly. "No. Everything in my room is still in one piece. I was talking about last night and Hayley."

"What about her? She was happier than I'd ever seen her."

She blew out a heavy breath and shoved her hair off her forehead. "Well, that's good, but not if it's at your expense. And last night I got the feeling that you weren't keen about the tree and all that stuff." Her eyelashes fluttered as she lifted her gaze to his face. "I'm sorry if I've forced you to do something you're not comfortable with. And what you give your daughter for Christmas is your business and I shouldn't be poking my nose where it doesn't belong."

"That's quite a speech."

"It wasn't a speech. It was an apology."

Boone had spent most of the night awake with his mind on this woman. She stirred him physically and reminded him how empty and cold his bed had been for the past ten years. She also made him think about himself, his daughter and the blind way he was stumbling through fatherhood.

Suddenly the urge to reach out and touch her was so strong he pushed himself to his feet and moved away from the table just to keep from giving in to it.

"The apology was unnecessary, Dallas," he muttered as he walked over to the cabinet counter and plunked down his empty mug.

"You're not…angry with me?"

Last night after he'd helped her and Hayley locate the decorations and lower them from the attic, he'd quickly excused himself and gone to his room for the night. He supposed Dallas had mistaken his disappearance for anger, but in actuality he'd simply been afraid if he stayed around her and Hayley much longer they would pull him into the Christmas merrymaking. And he didn't want that. Not when he knew the fun would be over just as soon as Dallas drove away from the ranch.

He glanced over his shoulder at her. "Angry? No. I was disappointed that you thought I was uninterested about Hayley's Christmas."

She shook her head with regret. "I spoke without thinking. Because…well, I can see for myself how much you love your daughter. It just annoyed me that you didn't make Christmas a more personal thing for her. It would mean so much if you'd take the time and trouble to pick out a special gift for her."

He turned so that he was facing her. "Damn it, I know that. But I wouldn't have a clue what to get her. Girls are so…different. Whatever I picked out, she'd hate."

"Why don't you try? You might be surprised."

He folded his arms against his chest. "I suppose your father is good at such things?"

She nodded. "He knows each of his children like a book. For instance, last Christmas he got me a diamond brooch fashioned in the shape of a running horse."

He frowned. "So you're telling me I should buy Hayley diamonds? She's a little young for that. Besides, I'm not exactly flush with money."

With a shake of her head, she got up from the table, and as she walked over to where he stood, Boone couldn't help but notice that the front of her robe was untied to reveal the silky fabric of her pajamas. The thin blue fabric fluttered against her curves and outlined the erotic shape of one perfect nipple.

"You're missing the whole message," she told him.

No, he was getting the message loud and clear, Boone thought. She was a hell of a sexy woman and he wanted her. But it wouldn't be smart to have her. So he was going to have to keep his eyes off her body and his mind steered clear of the delights she could give him.

"And what is that?" he asked.

She sighed as though she was disappointed that she had to explain. "The best gifts usually aren't those that have monetary value. Like love."

The moment her last word was out, he had to look away. Out of the whole dictionary, she had to pick a word that left him feeling naked and stupid and even a little angry.

"Sure. That sounds all rosy and perfect," he said with sarcasm. "Life is a rainbow and love conquers all. That may be enough for you, but I figure a twelve-year-old girl would rather have a pair of ripped jeans or an iPod full of music. At least I understand that much about females."

He glanced back around to see that her lips were pressed to a thin line.

"That cynical crap might ease your conscience, Boone, but it doesn't do anything to impress me."

He cocked a brow at her. "You think I'm trying to impress you?"

Her green eyes roamed his face. "I'm not sure what you're trying to do," she murmured.

Before Boone could stop himself, he closed the short distance between them and slipped his arms beneath the robe and around her waist. The contact caused her to let out a soft gasp and, in what felt like the gentle stroke of fingers, her warm breath brushed his cheek.

"I can tell you one thing. I know exactly what I *want* to do."

Surprise flickered in her eyes and then with a sense of dismay she whispered, "Boone."

"Yeah, I know. Yesterday morning I said I wasn't going to kiss you again. Ever. So call me a weak-willed bastard. A liar. Whatever you want to call me," he murmured. "It'll be worth it."

Her lips parted as though she was going to speak, but no words came out. Instead, she groaned and reached for him. As her soft curves pressed against him, she whispered, "Boone, this is insane. You don't know me. Not really. And I—"

He brought his forehead against hers. "You want this as much as I do," he finished for her.

Her hands flattened against his chest, then slid slowly upward until her fingers clamped over his shoulders. The fact that she was gripping him as though she never wanted to let go filled him with a strange mixture of hot desire and a tenderness he'd never quite felt before.

"I'm not— I don't do this sort of thing, Boone."

The fragrance of lilacs clung to her hair and the sweet, old-fashioned scent seemed perfectly sexy on her. He rubbed his cheek against her temple as the warmth of her body spread through his. "What does that mean? You don't kiss men?"

"Not a man I just met," she said in a breathy voice. "This is reckless behavior. And I'm not a reckless, impulsive person."

Beneath the silky fabric of her pajamas, her soft flesh yielded to his hands and he desperately longed to push the garment aside, to feel her satiny skin against his palms. But he didn't allow himself to take such a liberty. As she'd just said, they didn't know each other. And she was not the sort to give herself to just any man.

"Do you think this is normal behavior for me?" he asked lowly. "I can damned well tell you it isn't."

She moved her head just enough to rest her cheek against his and Boone was stunned by the hunger she evoked in him.

"Then what are we doing? Why is this happening?"

"I don't know. And I don't want to know," he said gruffly.

Unable to wait another second, his hand came up to capture her chin and he tugged her mouth around to his. The sweetness of her lips was everything he remembered and more, and though he tried to temper his desire, he couldn't slow the frantic search of his lips or the probe of his tongue.

This time it was Dallas who ended the kiss and as she backed out of his arms, he wiped a hand over his face and tried to douse the heat that was still burning his loins.

"I think—" She stopped and gulped in a deep breath of air. "I'd better go get dressed."

His body aching, he took a step toward her. "You

putting on clothes won't change anything," he hoarsely pointed out.

Pink color splashed across her white face. "And what would?" she countered. "Us falling to the floor and going at each other? Just to end the agony?"

He stepped close enough to reach for her hand and felt relief when she didn't pull her fingers away from his. "That's a crude thing to say."

Her nostrils flared and though he could see she was trying to hold on to her determined resistance, he could see a wavering look flicker in her eyes.

"That's because I'm feeling crude," she responded in a low, husky voice. "And stupid. And—and wishing I'd never stepped foot in this place!"

Yesterday, as they'd worked together, Boone had felt a kinship with this woman, a bond that he'd never felt before. And somewhere along the way, he'd let himself start to believe that she was different, that she might see and understand what he was about and why he chose to live as he did. Obviously, he'd been a fool to ever think she could be *that* different.

"I'm sure you probably are wishing you'd never left your paradise to come up here and get stuck in such a wasteland!"

Her eyes popped wide at the same time her mouth fell open. "It's not the land I'm having a problem with. It's the man who owns it!"

Before he could get a word pushed off his tongue, she jerked her hand free of his grasp and hurried out of the kitchen.

As Boone watched her disappear through the open doorway, her words echoed in his head.

For years he'd blamed the isolation of this ranch as

the main reason his marriage had failed. Now he had to wonder if the blame rested solely on his shoulders.

He wasn't a charmer or a Romeo. He wasn't a partier or traveler or even a decent conversationalist. He didn't have money or possess a list of valuable assets. Other than Hayley he didn't even have a family. Unless he counted his drunkard father, but Newt didn't want to be counted so that left him out.

So what did Boone have to offer a woman like Dallas? he asked himself.

Nothing, he thought with grim acceptance. Nothing at all.

Chapter Seven

By the time Dallas summoned up enough nerve to return to the kitchen, Boone was nowhere to be seen. A dirty plate in the sink told her he'd eaten something and gone on about his business.

Which was probably for the best, she told herself. If the two of them didn't keep a safe distance between them, something crazy was going to happen. And she didn't want to go home with a suitcase full of regrets.

She'd fixed herself a bowl of cereal and taken three bites when Hayley staggered into the kitchen.

"Goodness, I didn't expect you to be awake this early," Dallas said with surprise. "Since school is out I thought you'd be sleeping late."

Rubbing her eyes with both fists, Hayley yawned widely. "I do usually sleep until about seven-thirty or eight on the weekends, but today is different."

The child's comment brought a curious arch to Dallas's brows. "Oh? How so?"

Hayley held up two fingers as she walked to the refrigerator. "Two reasons. The first one is that you're here. And the second is that we're going after a Christmas tree. Remember?"

Oh, yes, she remembered too much, Dallas thought wryly. Her discussion with Boone about the Christmas tree and gifts had led to something she'd not anticipated.

Yesterday, after he'd made a big issue of vowing to never kiss her again, he'd turned around and done that very thing. He wasn't trying to hide the fact that he wanted her and yet he seemed to hate himself for it. The whole matter had left Dallas feeling confused and angry and more than a little worried. When she was around Boone, she couldn't seem to think with her head. And once he started touching her, she lost all will to resist.

"Yes. I remember."

"Where is Dad, anyway?" Hayley asked as she placed a packaged cinnamon role in the microwave.

In spite of the cold milk in her cereal, Dallas's lips began to burn with the memory of Boone's kiss. What would the girl think if she knew just how close Dallas had been to her father? Would she resent another female in his life?

It doesn't matter, Dallas. From what Hayley told you, Boone doesn't want another female in his life. Not likely on a permanent basis. He wants sex from you. Nothing more. The man won't even talk to you if it's not about horses.

"I don't know," she answered as casually as she could. "I suppose he's already gone outside to work. Does he usually leave the house this early? I mean, on the days you don't go to school."

"Sometimes. It just depends on if anybody is coming to buy horses. Or if him and Mick are gonna do extra work. Like round up some of the cows and give them shots or something like that."

The girl carried a glass of milk and her sugary sweet roll over to the table and sat down next to Dallas.

As Hayley began to eat, Dallas wanted to tell her she should be eating a hot breakfast full of protein and whole grains. But children her age weren't interested in such things. Besides, Dallas had no business trying to play mother to a child she'd never see again once she left this ranch.

"Have you known Mick for a long time?" Dallas asked.

"As long as I can remember. He and my dad have been friends forever. Since they were little kids."

"Does Mick have a wife and family?"

Hayley giggled as though that idea was extremely amusing. "No. Why? Do you think he's cute?"

Dallas practically gasped. "Hayley, that's a silly question."

She looked at Dallas and grinned. "I don't think it's silly. But I think my dad is the best-lookin', don't you?"

Dallas absently stirred her cereal as she tried to come up with a safe answer. "Well, both men are attractive," she answered carefully.

"Do you like to go on dates?"

Hayley's question was asked with a candor that only a child could possess.

"Sometimes," Dallas answered. "If I really like the guy."

The girl let out a wistful sigh. "I can't go on a date until I get sixteen. Dad's already set the rules. And that's a long time from now. I'll be getting old by then."

Dallas smiled to herself. "Fathers sometimes soften. Mine did. And perhaps Boone will allow you to go on a chaperoned date before you reach sixteen. At least that's something to hope for."

Eager light flickered in Hayley's brown eyes. "Do you think he might do that?" Without waiting for Dallas to respond, she shook her head. "Naw. Dad rarely ever gives in. And I don't have a mom to stand up for me."

Hayley's last remark wasn't said in a sad way or as a means to gain sympathy. It had simply been a matter-of-fact statement. And somehow that made this girl's situation seem even sadder to Dallas.

"My mom was always stricter than my dad," Dallas told her. "So having a mom around doesn't always mean you'll get your way."

"No. But it would be nice to have one, anyway."

Dallas thoughtfully stirred the last dregs of her cereal around in the bowl. "You know, it's just been you and your father for a long time. You might resent a woman coming between you," Dallas suggested.

"She'd have to be a mean person for me not to like her. And I don't think Dad would ever marry another mean woman. Shoot, I don't think he'll ever marry any woman again. So I guess it doesn't matter," she said with a shrug of one shoulder.

"No," Dallas murmured. "I guess it doesn't."

A half hour later, after they'd tidied the kitchen and Hayley had dressed in jeans and a thick sweatshirt, the two donned coats and sock caps and headed outside to the barn.

"I'll show you the horses that I picked out," Dallas said to the girl as they walked across the hard-packed earth.

"I hope they're not any of your favorites. I'd hate to think I was taking away a horse that you loved."

Although the morning sun was up, a cloak of clouds was beginning to cover the sky, making the morning even chillier. But Hayley seemed impervious to the cold. Every three or four steps she was skipping and smiling.

"I only have one favorite horse. And Dad keeps him separated. His name is Rock. I'll show him to you."

As they neared the main barn, Dallas noticed two different trucks parked alongside the building. She recalled one of them as belonging to Mick. The other she'd not seen before.

"Looks like your father has company. It may be a while before he can take us to get the tree," Dallas suggested.

Hayley grimaced. "We can't wait all day!" she exclaimed. "I have to get ready for the play tonight."

The two strode on into the barn and quickly ran into Mick, who was in the process of saddling a big sorrel horse.

"Well, good morning, ladies," he greeted with a wide grin. "What's brought you two out so early this morning?"

"We're looking for Dad," Hayley informed the ranch hand. "He's going to take me and Dallas to find a Christmas tree."

This caused the man to pause and settle a curious gaze on Dallas. "A Christmas tree? Are you kiddin' me?"

"Why, no. It is the Christmas season," Dallas politely reasoned.

"Well, yeah, but Boone—"

"Decided it would be a nice tradition for Hayley this year," Dallas added before he could say more. The poor girl already had enough rough, male influence in her life without adding more to it, she thought.

"Sure," the man replied, "Hayley's a good kid, aren't you, Button? You deserve a Christmas tree and a load of gifts beneath it."

"I don't want much of anything," Hayley told Mick, then reached over and clasped Dallas's hand as though she'd already been given the gift of her presence and that was enough. The idea caused Dallas's throat to tighten with raw emotions.

"Where's Dad? And where you goin'?" she asked Mick.

"Boone is showing horses to a customer. And I'm riding out to check a few feeders. But if you ladies don't want to wait around on Boone, I can drive you over to the bluffs to find a tree."

The guy didn't waste any time, Dallas thought. "Thank you, Mick. But I think this is something Boone wants to do with his daughter."

"I'm gonna go ask him when he'll be ready," Hayley announced.

Before either adult could stop her, the girl whirled and ran out of the barn.

Staring after her, Mick shook his head. "Boone won't like being disturbed. Hayley knows that."

At Hayley's age, Dallas had been a huge daddy's girl and trailed after Doyle like a puppy dog. And during that time, she'd learned, mostly the hard way, that men didn't want to be interrupted when they were in a serious conversation.

"She's excited," Dallas explained.

"Yeah. First time I've seen her like that since…well, her grandmother was alive."

He directed his startling blue eyes at her and Dallas thought she saw a look of faint accusation in them.

"Just what are you up to, Ms. Donovan?"

Totally stunned by his out-of-the-blue question, Dallas stared at him. "Excuse me? I'm afraid I don't understand."

"Really? You don't?"

The sarcasm in his voice suddenly painted a clear picture. This man didn't trust her and apparently believed that where Boone was concerned she had hidden motives. The idea was ludicrous.

"Ahh. I see," she said finally. "Well, you needn't worry about your friend. Boone and I have already made a deal for the horses. And though it's really none of your business, I paid him top dollar and was glad to do it. So if you thought I was trying to use my…uh, feminine charms to cheat him out of the horses, you couldn't be more wrong."

He barked out a laugh of amused disbelief. "Believe me, Dallas, it wasn't the horse deal I was thinking about."

She absently stroked the sorrel's nose as she looked at this man, who apparently considered himself Boone's protector. "Oh? Then what could possibly be on your mind? I'm just biding my time until my truck is repaired. I'm sorry if my presence bothers you, but I'll be gone soon. Maybe you should hang on to that thought so you won't be so worried about me carrying off the ranch," she added sarcastically.

Frowning, he looked away from her. "I'm sorry, Dallas. Forget I said any of this. It's not my way to behave like a bastard. But Boone isn't being himself and I'm worried about him."

"Why?"

He let out a long breath as he rested a forearm on the

sorrel's saddle. "There's no way you could know, but Boone went through a terrible time with his ex-wife."

"I do know."

This jerked his head around to Dallas. "You do? How—"

"How doesn't matter," Dallas replied. "I understand that things were difficult around here."

Mick swore softly. "*Difficult* wasn't the word for it. Joan was a mental wreck and she put Boone through hell. Oh, she wasn't that way in the beginning," he continued as though reading the questions in Dallas's mind, "but it didn't take long for her to unravel. But by then Boone was all wrapped up in her—especially after she got pregnant. He wanted things with her to work. In my opinion he hung on far too long."

Desperately trying to hang on to the woman he loved? Dallas wondered. Or had his main concern been for his daughter? Either way, she hated to think of such a strong man as Boone having to endure such a tragic situation.

"I don't think we should be discussing Boone's personal life," Dallas told him. "Besides, it has nothing to do with me."

"It shouldn't," Mick agreed. "But I think Boone is a bit taken with you."

Dallas mentally groaned. Was the simmering chemistry between her and Boone so obvious that this man could see it? "Taken with me? In what way?"

He looked at her. "I think he's attracted to you. And—"

The remainder of his thoughts went unsaid as Hayley came racing into the barn with Boone not far behind.

Clearing his throat, Mick quickly began to tighten the saddle cinch. Dallas stepped away from the horse and waited as Hayley, then Boone, reached her side.

"Dad's ready to go now, Dallas!" Hayley announced with excitement. "Are you?"

She glanced at Boone to see he was studying her and Mick with guarded speculation. The idea made Dallas want to curse. The two men were behaving as though they'd never seen a woman before, especially on this ranch. And maybe they hadn't, Dallas tried to fairly rationalize. With the drive from here to the nearest blacktopped highway taking nearly forty minutes, it wasn't like friends and neighbors were constantly popping by. Perhaps Dallas was an anomaly that had disturbed their mundane routine.

"Sure." She caught Boone's gaze with hers. "What about your customer?"

"He's coming back tomorrow and bringing a vet with him. He wants to make sure that whatever he buys is sound."

"Well to hell with him!" Mick exclaimed. "You should have run his a— You should have run him off the place."

Mick's blunt suggestion caused Boone to roll his eyes. "I don't care if he brings an army of vets out here. They'd find all the horses I have for sale are sound and healthy. Otherwise, they'd be sequestered away from the others. Anyway, I think he was a bit peeved because I refused to let him get near Midnight."

"Midnight?" Mick looked thoughtful. "I don't remember a horse around here by that name."

"The black stallion. He belongs to Dallas now."

The knowing glance that Mick directed at Dallas caused her cheeks to turn pink, but thankfully Boone didn't notice as he was already curling his arm around Hayley's shoulder and urging her out of the barn.

Dallas followed a step behind them.

* * *

The bluffs, a place that Mick had mentioned earlier, was a good five miles from the ranch house, and with no direct road to follow, Dallas got the impression that they were simply driving to another spot in the desert. But halfway there, the landscape began to change to low mountains and dry creek beds. Slabs of rock and jagged outcroppings suddenly appeared and the faint trail that Boone seemed to be following turned even rougher.

Each time they hit a rough bump Hayley laughed and bounced on the truck seat, while Dallas gripped the armrest for dear life.

"Too rough for you, Dallas?" Boone asked as he swerved to miss a huge clump of sage.

Dallas's body was thrown toward Hayley, who was sitting between the two adults and seemingly loving every minute of the ride.

"No. I'll just probably be black-and-blue in the morning," she joked as she struggled to straighten herself up in the seat. "I can certainly see why you drove this old ranch truck."

"Just hold on. We're almost there," he promised.

"It's really pretty, too, Dallas," Hayley added. "It's one of my favorite places on the ranch."

If Hayley missed some of the fun things her town friends enjoyed, she certainly wasn't showing it at the moment. Her expression was radiant as she glanced all about her. And as Dallas watched a myriad of emotions cross her sweet face, she could see a bit of herself in the young girl. The close bond Hayley had with her father, her love of animals and appreciation of the land that was her home were all traits that reminded Dallas of herself. The notion drew her even closer to the girl and when

Hayley suddenly turned a smile on her, Dallas's chest filled with a flood of maternal emotions.

The truck crested a steep incline and Dallas gasped at the same time Hayley instructed her to look at the panoramic view in front of them.

"Oh! There's a river! It's beautiful!" Dallas exclaimed.

Below them on the valley floor a strip of green vegetation followed the silver strip of water winding across the desert. "That's the White. The river that the ranch is named after," Boone informed her.

Dallas leaned eagerly up in her seat. "It's like an oasis," she said with awe. "Are we going down there?"

"Not to cut a tree," Boone answered. "But we can go down later for a look, if you'd like."

Hayley bounced with excitement. "Oh, yes, Dad! That'd be great!"

"You should first be asking our guest what she would like to do, Hayley," Boone instructed his daughter.

The girl twisted around to Dallas. "It'd be okay with you, wouldn't it?"

Dallas smiled at her. "I'd love to."

Boone drove along the top of the ridge for a short distance until he found a flat spot to park the old Ford. Afterward, he collected an ax from the bed of the truck and the three of them walked along the top of the bluff, where thick stands of juniper and pinyon grew from the loamy soil.

"There's no spruce around here," Boone told Dallas as the two of them strolled abreast of each other. "To find one of those we'd have to go much farther north and we don't exactly have time for that today."

Dallas shook her head. "One of these trees will be just as beautiful. It's the symbol of the tree that's most important. And I think Hayley gets that."

Boone gazed ahead to where his daughter was skipping and racing from tree to tree. "She's enjoying this much more than I ever thought." He glanced over at Dallas. "It makes me feel like I've been neglecting her. And I don't like that. I don't want to be anything like Newt. It makes me sick to my stomach to think that I might be turning into a man like him."

"Newt?"

"Yeah. My dad," he said bluntly.

Since Dallas knew very little about his parents, it was hard for her to understand the disdain she heard in Boone's voice. She could only surmise that something about Newt Barnett and his family had gone very wrong.

"You haven't been a neglectful father, Boone. I can see that."

The grateful look he cast her touched her as much as any smile could have, because he didn't seem like the sort of man who needed or wanted approval from anyone. The fact that he appreciated hers made Dallas feel somewhat special.

He said, "Being a parent…it's not easy to do everything the right way. One of these days you'll find that out for yourself."

Her heart winced as she bit back a wistful sigh. Would she ever know what it was like to be a mother? These past few years, since the debacle with Allen, she'd often wondered if a man—the right man—would ever come into her life. But Boone couldn't be that man. To let her thoughts even go in that direction would be futile.

"Maybe," she said solemnly. "Someday."

His steps came to a halt and as he turned to Dallas, she paused to meet his gaze head-on. Was that regret or longing that flickered in his eyes? Either way, she felt her heart melt just a little.

"Dallas, this morning—"

He stopped, clearly uncertain about what he wanted to say. But Dallas didn't have any trouble softly admitting, "I said some things without thinking."

"So did I."

She swallowed as emotions swelled in her throat. "Something happens to me, Boone, whenever I'm close to you."

"Yes," he said gently. "It happens to me, too."

"What are we going to do about it?" she asked.

He was about to speak when Hayley called out to them from a few yards away.

"Hey, you two! Come look at this pine! It's looks really perfect!"

His lips took on a wry slant. "Sounds like we're being summoned."

Dallas nodded. "Yes. And this outing is for Hayley."

He started walking toward his daughter and Dallas joined him. Once they reached Hayley, Boone took great pains to look over the size and shape of the tree before he aptly declared it a beauty.

A few swings of Boone's axe brought the tree quickly down and after he shouldered it, the three of them headed back to the truck. Along the way, Hayley reached for Dallas's hand and the silent connection filled her with a warm, maternal feeling, a protectiveness that went far beyond her normal reaction to children.

First the man and now his daughter, she thought desperately. If she wasn't careful, before she left this ranch, the two of them were going to take over her heart completely.

Once at the truck, Boone loaded the tree and as the three of them started to climb back into the cab, Hayley insisted that she wanted to ride next to the window.

Dallas wondered if Hayley's request had anything to with getting a better view or if she was subtly trying to throw Dallas and Boone together. Either way, she didn't argue with the girl. Instead she climbed in and settled herself in the middle of the bench seat and tried her best not to notice that her thigh was crammed against Boone's and each time the truck swayed, her shoulder brushed his.

"I think I see a few snowflakes in the air," Boone commented as he headed the truck off the ridge and toward the river. "That's a surprise."

"What if it snows a lot, Dad? I've got to get to church tonight for the play, remember?"

"I've not forgotten. But it's highly unlikely that we'll see *any* snow, much less get snowed in."

Sitting in the middle forced Dallas's legs to straddle the stick shift in the floor, but Boone's hand resting on the knob was the thing that was getting to her the most.

This morning that same hand had touched her, caressed her, heated her like no flame could have. Or no other man ever had, she thought. The realization didn't just surprise her, it troubled her.

"Well, it still might not hurt if we went to town earlier, Dad? We could eat out for dinner at the Mine Shaft. That way it wouldn't matter how much it snowed."

Boone cut Dallas a look of wry amusement. "My daughter doesn't know how to give hints. She just comes out and says what she wants."

"Sort of like her father, I think," Dallas couldn't help but say.

Ignoring Dallas's remark, he said to Hayley, "We'll see."

Hayley didn't press him for a more concrete answer and that alone impressed Dallas. Clearly the girl didn't get anything and everything she wanted, yet she respected her father enough not to hound, beg or argue. Boone had said, as a parent, he'd made mistakes with Hayley, but if that was the case, he'd certainly made up for them in other ways, she thought.

"So you don't get snowed in on the ranch very often?" Dallas asked.

Boone shook his head. "It's rare that we ever see a sprinkling of snow. The past few years it's been extremely dry around here."

"We can always hope, Dad," Hayley said as she focused her gaze out the window. "See! There goes a few flakes now!"

Boone exchanged a private grin with Dallas. "Yes, we can hope, princess. A long time ago we had winters with lots of snow. But that was back…before my grandparents were killed."

The wistful note in his voice tugged on Dallas's heart and without thinking she reached over and laid her hand on his knee.

"I wish I could have met them."

He cast a brief look of regret at her. "I wish you could have, too," he said gently.

The truck bounced forward for several yards before Dallas realized her hand was still resting on his knee. She hastily pulled it back, then darted a glance at Hayley. Thankfully the girl was still staring out the passenger window and had missed the caring touch she'd given Boone. Not that there had been anything inappropriate about the gesture, Dallas reasoned. But she'd been getting the feeling that Hayley would like for something to develop between her father and Dallas and she didn't want to feed into the girl's childish dreams. Hayley was craving a mother, or at least, a mother figure. It would be heartless to let the girl think Dallas could ever be that mother.

This brief time with Boone and Hayley would end in two or three days, at the most. After that she'd be back in New Mexico and this man and his young daughter would be nothing more than a memory.

Or would they?

Chapter Eight

Once the three of them returned to the ranch and ate a light lunch, Boone erected the tree in the family room, then hung around for a few more minutes until Dallas and Hayley got busy pulling out strings of lights, garland and ornaments to decorate the huge pine.

"It looks like the tree is going to stay upright, so you two don't need me anymore," he said, as he pulled on his coat and reached for his hat.

"But Dad, don't you want to help us decorate?" Hayley implored.

"That's a job for you and Dallas," he told his daughter. "I've got more work to finish at the barns before we leave for town."

"Okay," Hayley conceded. "We'll have it looking really pretty by the time you come back in."

Pausing at the doorway of the room, he shoved back the sleeve of his coat to glance at his watch. "I'll try to be back here at the house by four o'clock. So you girls need to be ready shortly after that. We'll go early and have dinner at the Mine Shaft—if that suits the two of you."

As far as Hayley was concerned, his announcement certainly compensated for not being around for the tree decorating. She immediately began to bounce on her toes and clap her hands. "Yes, Dad! That'll be great!"

With a humorous twist to his lips, he cast a questioning look at Dallas. "What about you? Are you up to a bit of bright lights and big city?"

The teasing note she heard in his voice surprised Dallas. He was not the sort of man that joked. The fact that he was exhibiting any sort of playfulness told her that he was actually looking forward to the evening ahead.

The idea filled her with anticipation and she smiled back at him.

"I'm ready for anything."

Are you? The question was clearly in his eyes and Dallas was wondering what in the world had possessed such a remark to come out of her mouth, when he suddenly slapped his hat on his head and headed out the door.

Later that evening, Dallas dressed in a long black skirt and a thin red sweater with ruffles edging the wrists and the V neckline. When she'd initially packed for the trip, her plan had been to be gone from the Diamond D for no more than three days, so she'd kept her wardrobe to a minimum. But thankfully, at the last moment, she'd tossed in the skirt and sweater, just in case it might be needed. Little had she known that she'd be attending dinner and a Christmas play with a man who made her heart stutter and stammer every time he got within ten feet of her.

She was fastening a simple silver cross and chain at the back of her neck, when Hayley knocked on the bedroom door and quickly stepped inside.

"Is it okay if I come in?" she asked.

Dallas looked at her and smiled. "Sure. Do you need help with anything?"

Hayley stood before her and held out her arms. "Do I look like a geek in this? I wear jeans all the time and this is something a friend gave me that she didn't want anymore."

The little flared velvet skirt in deep purple coupled with a trendy vest to match made Hayley look like a different child. "Oh, you look so pretty, Hayley! That looks great."

Wrinkling her nose with uncertainty, Hayley looked down at herself. "At the play, I'll have an angel robe that will cover everything up, so I guess it don't matter much what I have on now. But I wanted to look nice for dinner. We don't... Well, we go out and eat sometimes, but we—" Pausing, she glanced up, her eyes suddenly gleaming as she smiled at Dallas. "We've never had a guest with us. Especially a beautiful lady like you."

Hayley's comment not only touched Dallas, but also told her a few things about Boone. He didn't venture off the ranch on a regular basis. And he didn't date. Neither fact surprised her, but both of them troubled her. He was a man who had so much to offer a woman, yet he obviously didn't want to share himself with one. Nor did he believe he needed a steady connection to people or the outside world. He was either hiding from life, she thought, or refusing to join in. And either reason was not acceptable to her.

"Thank you, Hayley. I'm very honored to join you and your father tonight."

Still not completely sure of her appearance, Hayley moved closer to Dallas and stuck one foot forward. "These are the only dressy shoes I have," she declared.

The ballerina flats were appropriate for Hayley's age, but not the weather. "They look nice, but your feet are going to freeze. I heard on the weather forecast that the temperature will be in the teens tonight. Do you have a pair of boots?"

"Cowboy boots. That's all."

"Well, why not wear them? That's what I'm wearing. See?" Dallas lifted her skirt so that Hayley could see her black boots.

"Gee, that looks neat."

"Thanks. They're all I brought with me on this trip so I hope they look neat. I wasn't expecting to be going out for an evening like this," Dallas explained.

"Wait a minute! I'll be right back!"

Hayley rushed out of the room and Dallas turned back to the dresser and reached for a hairbrush. She was twisting up her red waves and clipping them to her head, when the girl raced back into the bedroom and skidded to a halt in the middle of the floor.

"Now look! What do you think?" she asked as she turned full circle for Dallas's inspection.

Even though Dallas was trying her best not to feel like a mother, she did and a wealth of love and protectiveness flooded through her as she walked over to Hayley and gave her a brief hug. "I think we look like twins and we're going to knock everybody's eyes out tonight."

Giggling, Hayley hugged her back. "Wow! This is gonna be a special night."

* * *

A special night indeed, Dallas thought later, as they
neared Pioche and the lights of town glittered against the
stark desert backdrop. Even though the tiny old mining
town only boasted a population of around nine hundred
people, Boone and Hayley seemed to consider it a busy
metropolis. And compared to the isolation of White River
Ranch, it was that and more. After spending three days
on the lonely ranch, Dallas felt as if she was actually returning to civilization.

But it wasn't just the chance of seeing busy towns-
folk and businesses decorated for the Christmas season
that was making it special for Dallas. Behind the wheel,
Boone was handsomely dressed in a white shirt and dark
brown Western-cut suit that set off his sun-streaked hair
and dark tan. But the best part of his appearance was the
frequent smiles he'd been tossing her way. She'd not expected him to be enjoying this outing and she wondered
if she might be a part of the reason for his jovial mood.

Don't go there, Dallas. The man isn't falling for you.
He isn't thinking of having you for long-term company.
So forget it. Get your mind back on your family at home
and all that you're missing right now on the Diamond D.

The pestering little voice in her head was telling
her exactly how things really were and yet, for once in
her life, she couldn't focus on her family back home.
Boone's presence was so large it kept crowding away all
thoughts…except him.

"Do you have your voice limbered up for the play?"
Boone asked his daughter while he guided the double
cab truck down the simple main street of Pioche. "Maybe
you'd better drink something warm at dinner to get your
vocal chords loosened up."

From her place in the backseat, Hayley groaned good-naturedly. "Oh, Dad. I've been talking all day to Dallas. My vocal chords are already warmed up."

He exchanged a meaningful look with Dallas, then winked. "I'm sure you have talked Dallas's ears off," he said to Hayley. "Now after hearing your chatter all day, she has to listen to you sing."

"And I'm very much looking forward to it," Dallas interjected.

"You shouldn't be. 'Cause I can't really sing," Hayley warned her. "I only got the part of an angel because I can hit high notes."

"Well, if you can hit high notes then you can surely sing," Dallas assured her. "Besides, enthusiasm is more important than perfection."

"Gosh, you sound just like my choir teacher."

Dallas chuckled at that thought and Boone asked, "Do you have nieces or nephews Hayley's age?"

"No. They're all kindergarten-age and younger. Why?"

He shrugged. "Just curious. You seem to understand her."

"I work with kids all day long. All week long," she explained. "After a while you learn them."

"Is that it?" he asked wryly. "I've had Hayley for more than twelve years and I'm not sure I've gotten the hang of understanding her yet."

On the south edge of town, Boone parked the truck in front of a large two-story building constructed of lumber that hadn't seen paint in more years than she'd been living. At one time, when the silver and nickel mines had been booming in the area, the building had served as a company store for the miners. Now it was a restaurant called the Mine Shaft.

Inside, a hostess seated the three of them at a round table covered with a white tablecloth. Once they were all settled, Dallas looked around her with curious appreciation. The interior of the eating place looked like something out of the Wild West days. The floor and walls consisted of bare wood while heavy beams crisscrossed the low ceiling. A long polished bar lined one long wall, while across the room an upright piano was currently being played by an elderly gentleman wearing a black wool vest and bowler hat. A few feet away from their table, a large window overlooked the dark desert and star-studded sky.

Dallas was surprised to see several people, mostly men, sitting at the bar enjoying drinks while the tables around them were all occupied with hungry diners.

"Is this place always this busy?" Dallas asked, after a waitress had taken their orders.

"It's Friday night and the weekend has started," Boone explained.

"It has a quaint charm," she told him. "I like it."

Hayley wrinkled her nose. "The food is okay. But this place is stuffy and for old people like you and Dad. I'd like to go some place where they have good music and you can get fries and milk shakes and pizza."

"You can order those things here, Hayley," Boone pointed out. "And if I remember right, you were the one so keen on coming here tonight to eat."

The girl tilted her head from one shoulder to the other as she contemplated her father's remark. "Well, yeah, I did," she allowed. "But that because it's the only decent restaurant in town. And it's better than eating at home. Besides, having Dallas with us makes it a lot more fun."

Boone turned his gaze on Dallas. "Yes. Everything is more fun with Dallas," he said.

Was he being serious or sarcastic? There was nothing on his face or in his voice to tell her which and Dallas spent the rest of the meal wondering what had been behind his remark and why it should even matter to her. Just because he looked like a rugged, sexy dream didn't make him the right man for her. And the fact that he was a hardworking, honorable man shouldn't sway her feelings, either. There were plenty of decent, good-looking, hardworking men back in Ruidoso and one of these days she'd find one.

Yeah, but he wouldn't kiss you like Boone. He wouldn't make you feel like you'd flown to the moon and back.

A flight to the moon wasn't what she needed, Dallas argued with the war of words tumbling around in her head. All she needed to fix her problem was a truck. Once she got back on the highway and headed home to New Mexico, she'd be fine. Boone could go on raising his daughter without the help of a wife, just as he had for the past twelve years. And Hayley…well, the girl could probably see the writing on the wall even clearer than Dallas. She was never going to get a stepmother.

The church was located on a hill overlooking town and as they neared the sloped parking area, it was obvious that there would be a big crowd on hand.

"Wow! Everybody is already here!" Hayley exclaimed as Boone searched for an empty parking space.

"Looks like it," he said as he stopped the truck and killed the motor. "Are you going to be late?"

Hayley flung off her seat belt and scrambled for the door. "No. I have five minutes. But I better hurry!"

Before Boone could say anything else, Hayley was on the ground and racing toward a side entrance of the church. With a shake of his head, he said, "She doesn't think too much of time until she realizes at the last minute that she's going to be late."

"She was enjoying her meal and wanted to linger," Dallas reasoned.

Grinning faintly, he said, "Yeah. Even if it wasn't fries and pizza."

He reached for Dallas's hand and quickly helped her out of the truck. Once they were on the ground, she expected him to release his hold on her. But he surprised her by keeping his hand firmly wrapped around hers as the two of them headed toward the church with a much slower gait than Hayley had taken.

The white stucco structure was L-shaped with a tall steeple erected over the front entrance and a row of beautiful stained-glass windows running along the sides. A priest was standing outside the door to greet church members and guests and it wasn't until they approached the middle-aged man that Boone finally released Dallas's hand.

"Good evening, Boone. Good to see you here. Is our little Hayley ready to perform?"

Boone's smile was full of fatherly pride. "Let's hope she is." With his hand at Dallas's back he urged her forward. "Father O'Quinn, I'd like for you to meet my friend. This is Dallas Donovan from New Mexico."

The kindly faced priest instantly offered his hand to Dallas. "Donovan? That's a nice Irish name," he said with a wink for her. "And how lovely you are!"

"Thank you, Father. It's very nice to meet you. My parents have dear friends back in Ireland by the name of O'Quinn. Perhaps you're related."

He kindly patted the top of her hand, while turning a pointed look on Boone. "You must bring Ms. Donovan by the rectory for a nice chat one day soon."

Boone awkwardly cleared his throat. "It would have to be very soon. Dallas will be leaving in the next two or three days."

"Oh." The priest appeared disappointed by the news, but when he turned back to Dallas, he bestowed her with a gentle reassuring smile that made her wonder if he could sense the turmoil that was beginning to build in her heart. "Just remember, Ms. Donovan, a road always travels both ways."

"Thank you, Father. I'll remember."

Inside the church, they found a seat on one of the long wooden pews. As Dallas settled next to him, he could only imagine what was going through Father O'Quinn's mind. For more years than Boone wanted to think about, the man had been urging him to remarry and build a family. No doubt, he'd clearly seen Dallas as wife mate-rial for Boone. But then, Father Aiden O'Quinn believed in miracles. And that's just what it would take for Dallas to ever become Mrs. Boone Barnett, he thought dismally.

The Christmas program, made up of a cast of chil-dren only, turned out to be a beautiful spectacle with the manger scene surrounded by real animals. When Hayley and three more winged angels appeared to sing joyful hymns, Boone had been filled with immense pride and love for his daughter. He'd also felt something more—something deep and bittersweet—as Dallas had momen-tarily reached over and covered his hand with hers as though she'd wanted to share the special moment with him.

Now, as they drove home in the quiet night, Boone re-alized he was treading on dangerous ground. He didn't know when or how it had happened, but at some point he'd stopped thinking of Dallas as a guest, as a horse buyer and nothing more. He could only think of her as a beautiful, desirable woman. A woman who made his daughter happy, and a woman who filled up the loneliness in his heart.

"I think Hayley has fallen asleep," Dallas remarked as the lights of the ranch house finally came into view.

"No. I'm not asleep." The girl sat up on the edge of the seat and yawned. "But I'm pretty tired. I didn't know acting was so exhausting."

"You weren't acting," Boone corrected. "You were singing."

"Well, I was acting like I could sing," the girl countered.

"You sounded beautiful," Dallas assured her. "I heard all the high notes."

Boone parked the truck at the back of the house and as they started toward the porch, Queenie ran up to greet them, then trotted along at Dallas's side as though she'd lived there for years rather than days.

Damned dog, Boone thought. She wasn't any smarter than he was.

When they entered the kitchen, Hayley yawned again and quickly excused herself for bed. But before she got halfway out of the room, she turned and rushed back to Dallas.

Boone stood awkwardly to one side as his daughter flung her arms around Dallas's waist and hugged her tightly.

"Thank you coming to see the play, Dallas. It felt really nice to know you were watching," she said.

Dallas bent her head and kissed the top of Hayley's head. "It felt really nice to be there," she assured the girl.

Hayley smiled up at her, then quickly left the room.

Once the girl was out of sight, Boone let out a long breath.

"I want to thank you, too," he said lowly. "For making a special effort to be kind to my daughter."

Dallas shook her head and for the hundredth or more time tonight, he could only think how beautiful and feminine she looked in her long skirt and with her hair coiled up on her head. The diamonds dangling from her ears glittered like real gems and he realized they most likely were. The expensive jewelry was a reminder that she lived more than a thousand miles away from him. She lived a world away from him.

"I didn't have to make any effort. Hayley is easy to love."

Easy to love. At one time in his life Boone had found it easy to love people. But that had all changed as, one by one, he'd lost those that he'd cared about the most. For years now he'd done his best to keep his heart shut tight toward anything or anyone, except for Hayley. His love for his daughter would never change. Then there were the horses, so wild and frightened at first and then so trusting and giving once they'd bonded with him. He kept more of them than he should, simply because it hurt too much to see them leave.

Now there was Dallas. And with each minute that ticked away he was beginning to feel the pain of loss looming ahead of him. He didn't want to like her, want or need her. And he damned well didn't want to love her. But something about her was turning him into a softhearted fool.

"That's nice of you to say," he said huskily, then cleared his throat, stepped around her and walked over to the cabinets. "I think I'll have a cup of coffee before I go to bed. Want one?"

"Sure. I'll find some cookies or something to go with it."

A few short minutes later Boone carried a tray with their drinks and snacks to the family room. While he placed the refreshments on the coffee table in front of the couch, Dallas plugged in the lights on the Christmas tree.

"We might as well enjoy the lights while we drink our coffee," Dallas said as she sank down on the couch, a cushion away from his.

He looked over at the decorated pine as mixed emotions rolled through him. "There hasn't been a Christmas tree in this house since my mother was alive," he admitted.

"Yes. Hayley told me."

He grimaced as he reached for a cookie. "She wasn't the best of mothers. But she tried in her own way. I miss her."

"I'm sure you do," she murmured, then asked, "Do you mind telling me what she was like?"

He shrugged. "She was one of those free-spirited types. A carryover, you might say, from the flower child era of the sixties. The only thing that anchored her was Newt, which never made sense. There's not a solid, dependable cell in my father's body. But she loved him blindly and in spite of his problems with alcohol."

He could feel her green eyes studying him thoughtfully and their touch disturbed him. "Is that why you don't get along with the man? Because of his drinking?"

"Mainly. But mostly because he shunned his responsibility as a father."

"So you think he never loved you."

Boone let out a cynical grunt. "I'm not sure if Newt is capable of loving anyone but himself." Turning his head, he locked his gaze with hers. "By the time I was five, my grandparents could see that I wasn't being raised in a normal family atmosphere and they literally took me out of my parents' house and into theirs."

"You think that was the right thing for them to do?"

Her question had him looking at her with amazement. "Right? Hell, I'm glad someone stepped up to care for me. Half the time we had no electricity in the house because Newt didn't work enough to pay the bill. I remember having meals of nothing but jelly beans and potato chips. And in winter the house would be so cold my mother would constantly cough."

With a rueful shake of her head, she half whispered, "I can't imagine you living as a child in those conditions, Boone. And I guess I don't understand, either. Why did Newt not try to do better?"

His gaze dropped to the steaming brown liquid in his cup. "Who knows why anyone turns worthless? But I think he wasn't always that way. From what I've gathered, my father and grandfather got into it when Newt was a teenager and they still lived in Arizona. He wanted the family to stay there, where Burt, my grandfather, made good money as a miner. He balked at the idea of his parents getting a ranch out in the middle of nowhere in Nevada."

"I remember you saying that your father didn't care for ranching. I take it that didn't change over the years."

Grimacing, he sipped his coffee. "No. Newt left home as soon as he was legally able, but he didn't move back to Arizona. He married Elsa and they lived in Reno until I was born, then they showed up in Pioche. Because they needed money, or so my grandparents told me."

"Did they give it to him?" Dallas asked, then shook her head. "I'm sorry. I keep asking you these personal questions. You don't have to tell me if it bothers you to talk about it."

He let out a cynical grunt. "What difference does it make now? You've already heard my family's dirty laundry. And to answer your question, yes, they made the mistake of giving him money—because of me. They wanted me cared for. But in the end they could see that their son was using me and them. So they took charge of me and cut off Newt from any financial aid."

"Any way you look at it…well, it must have been an awful situation," Dallas remarked.

He sighed. "Yeah. And when my grandparents were killed Newt was right there demanding the will be read and his part dished out to him. He threw a hell of a fit when he learned he had no part. Burt and Elsa had cut him out completely and willed everything to me."

Disbelief parted her lips. "Oh, my. I'll bet that has caused some problems between the two of you."

"I was fifteen at the time, so the ranch wasn't legally handed over to me until I was twenty-one. Before the transfer happened Newt did his best to persuade me to sell this place and give him part of the money."

"Hmm. Why did he think he deserved it?"

Boone tried to chuckle but the sound was more like a sickened gag. "He's always moaned about sacrificing everything he'd ever wanted when he had to leave Arizona. I'm not exactly sure what it was that he wanted so much—but he claims the move ruined his life. Anyway, Newt believed that gave him a right to inherit something."

"But obviously you didn't want to sell."

"Not on your life," he muttered. "My grandparents worked their rears off to make this place go. It was their life. And I've made it mine, too."

"Yes. I can see that."

His gaze swept back to her face. "You think that's a crime or something?"

A wan smile tilted her lips as she shook her head. "Not at all. I just meant that I can see where your devotion lies."

He let out a heavy breath, then shook his head. "Maybe I seem greedy to you, Dallas. After all, there's a lot of land with this ranch. I could sell part of it and give the money to Newt. But what would that accomplish? He'd simply drink it away and kill himself more quickly in the process. I can't see that being a smart move on my part."

Her gaze fell to her lap. "No," she said with a sigh, "that wouldn't be smart at all. I just wish—" She glanced up at him. "There was some way you two could patch up your differences. Do you visit with him at all?"

He placed his mug back on the tray. "Funny, isn't it, you'd think I'd find it easy to completely turn my back on him. But I can't. Whenever I drive into town, I usually drop by to check in on him. I tell myself I'm doing it for my mother. But deep down, I guess there's a part of me that wishes someday I'll walk in and find him a changed man."

A gentle smile tilted her lips and Boone's gaze automatically zeroed in on them just as they had for most of the night. The taste of her, the feel of her, was haunting his senses and all he wanted to do was pull her into his arms and let himself forget every word, every wall that stood between them.

"Change is hard for some people. And Newt probably believes he can't be any other way than what he is. Does he have anything to do with Hayley?"

"I won't let her go around him unless he's been off

the hooch for a day or two. So that's not very often. She loves him simply because he's her grandfather and about the only other relative, other than me, that she has. But I... It doesn't come that easy for me."

His restless thoughts pushed him to his feet and without thinking he walked over to the twinkling Christmas tree. The sight of it warmed him. Or was it Dallas's presence making everything seem special?

He looked over his shoulder at her and as he did, the telephone sitting near her elbow caught his eye. Since lunch, he'd not bothered to check his messages. For all he knew, horse clients were waiting on a return call from him.

"Did you check the answering machine this evening before we left for town?" he asked as he strode back over to where she sat.

"Why, no. I wouldn't feel right listening to your personal messages," she told him.

"I never receive a message that personal," he assured her, then punched the play button on the machine.

Three messages had been left. The first one by a woman looking to purchase a buckskin mare. The second was Marti, informing Dallas that the part for her truck had arrived, but the company had shipped him the wrong one. He'd ordered another pump and expected it to arrive tomorrow afternoon. The third call was from Dallas's sister-in-law, Lass.

"Hi, Dallas! Did Fiona give you the news about the babies? Brady is over the moon—especially with Johnny and Bridget expecting at the same time!" She giggled, then said, *"Grandmother Kate says if this keeps up, she's moving out to the horse barn. But all joking aside, things are great here. All the kids rode yesterday and I remembered to put Peter on Tumbleweed. We're getting ready*

*for the employee party tomorrow night. I hope you can
be home by then. Gosh, I miss you so much! Love you,
Dallas. Bye."*

The recorder clicked off and Boone looked down to
see Dallas wiping fingers beneath her eyes. The display
of emotion not only surprised him, but it also stabbed
him right in the middle of his chest.

"Dallas, are you crying?"

She sniffed and did her best to offer him a wobbly
smile. "I'm sorry, Boone. I don't usually sprout wa-
terworks. And I understand they grate on a man." She
drew in a deep breath and let it out. "It's just that hearing Lass's voice...got to me."

Moving around the coffee table, he sank down on the
cushion next to her and reached for her hand. "You're
homesick."

"Maybe a little," she conceded, then looked almost
apologetic. "But I'm enjoying my time here, Boone.
Please don't think that I'm not. This day has been wonderful. Getting the tree this morning. Our dinner and the
play tonight. I'll never forget any of it," she added huskily.

"Neither will I—ever forget," he admitted.

Her misty green eyes searched his face and he wondered why it felt like something or someone was squeez-
ing his heart.

"Really?"

Suddenly Boone couldn't fight himself any longer.
He tugged on her hand and she fell forward and into his
arms.

"Oh, Dallas...Dallas. None of this is supposed to be
happening. You'll be going soon. And I can't follow. But
while you're here—" He pressed his cheek against hers.

"I keep telling myself that it's okay to want you. Like this."

He found her mouth with his and as her lips opened and her arms slid around him, he realized that he was not the same man she'd met two nights ago.

When he ended the contact of their lips and began to trail a track of kisses down the side of her neck, she whispered, "This scares me, Boone. Really scares me. When I leave this ranch I don't want to leave my heart here with you."

"And I don't want you to leave it with me." Forcing the words through his tight throat, he rubbed his cheek against the skin bared by the V of her sweater. "Because I—I would only break it. Ruin it. And I never want to hurt you, sweet Dallas. Never."

Her fingers dipped into his hair and clamped against his scalp. Boone lifted his head to look at her and as their gazes met he groaned with sheer longing.

"Then kiss me and tell me good-night," she implored. "Otherwise, I might forget all the reasons we can't be together."

He searched her eyes while foolishly wondering why he couldn't have met her many years ago before the patterns of their lives had already been set, before he'd become a hollow man.

"And what are those reasons?" he had to ask, even though he already knew how she would answer.

"A thousand miles," she said sadly. "My home and family. And that's just for starters."

Everything inside of him suddenly felt heavy and dying. "A thousand miles," he repeated softly, then before he could change his mind, he pressed a gentle kiss upon her lips. "Good night, Dallas."

She stared at him for a moment, her eyes shadowed

with something like disappointment, and then suddenly she pulled herself from his arms and hurried out of the room.

Boone sat where he was for several minutes before he finally managed to push himself to his feet. The twinkling lights on the tree seemed to mock him and with a heavy heart he quickly turned them off and left the room.

On the way to his bedroom, the slit of light beneath Dallas's door beckoned to him and for a moment he paused and reconsidered his decision to tell her goodnight.

If he pushed, she would give. But in the end that wouldn't make him feel good about himself.

No, he had to put wanting her out of his mind. Like he'd told her, he'd made this ranch his life. And he couldn't give it up. Not even for her.

Chapter Nine

Dallas spent a fitful night trying to force herself to fall asleep. But at the most, she'd gotten only broken naps that had made her feel even groggier the next morning.

When she staggered into the kitchen it appeared that Boone had already been there and gone. Dallas was glad. Facing him this early was not how she needed to start her day.

Shoving back her heavy hair, she walked over to the coffeepot. After she poured herself a cup and took a careful sip, she gazed down the cabinet at the black phone attached to the wall.

Oh, God, how she missed her cell phone and the convenience of calling her family and friends anytime she wanted or needed them.

She missed the hustle and bustle of the Diamond D, the ranch hands and horses, jockeys, grooms and hot walkers. She missed the sound of the thundering hooves as the colts and fillies galloped the track. But mostly she missed her family, her riding stables and the children. Everything that was important to her was back in New Mexico.

And yet so much of her was dreading the day she would have to leave this quiet and lonely ranch. It didn't make sense, but the feelings were there anyway.

After a quick breakfast she dressed in jeans and a heavy gray sweater, then as she stepped outside topped it with her denim ranch jacket.

On the way to the barns she noticed the sky had cleared and the wind had calmed somewhat. It was going to be a beautiful day, she decided, even if her heart was all mixed-up inside.

She was behind one of the smaller barns, checking over the six horses she'd purchased, when Hayley came trotting across the dusty corral.

"Dallas, where's Dad? I've looked all over and can't find him."

From the rapid rise and fall of her chest, the girl had obviously run all the way out here. "Is something wrong?" Dallas asked quickly.

"No. Well, sorta. I need to ask him something. And I don't have much time. I gotta find him. Is Mick around? Maybe he knows where Dad is."

"I haven't seen either one of them. Is there anything I can do to help you?"

Hayley released a dramatic sigh. "My best friend, Jennifer, has invited me to go with her and her family to Las Vegas on a Christmas shopping trip. They're gonna spend the night there and go to a movie and all that cool kind of stuff."

The girl's obvious excitement brought a smile to Dallas's face. "That sounds like lots of fun. Do you think your father will give you permission to go?"

The girl tilted her head from one side to the other. "I don't know. He's stricter than my friends' fathers, but sometimes he lets me go places. But this time...I just gotta go! I could pick out something for Dad's Christmas present without him seeing and—"

She stopped in midsentence as a troubled look fell over her face.

"What's wrong?" Dallas asked quickly.

"I just remembered. You'll probably get your truck back tomorrow and then you'll leave the next morning, and if I go to Vegas with Jennifer I'll miss being here—with you."

In spite of the heaviness in Dallas's heart, she gave the girl a reassuring smile. "Oh, honey, you don't want to miss the opportunity to take a trip just because of me. Christmas is coming! It's a time to do special things."

She studied Dallas for a thoughtful moment. "You mean, you think I should go for it?"

Bending, Dallas tenderly cupped her gloved hands around Hayley's face. "It would make me happy for you to go and have fun." She swallowed as more emotions tightened her throat. "And who knows, maybe I'll be coming back someday to buy more horses and we'll get to see each other again."

"Oh, yeah. That would be great. Or maybe I could talk Dad into driving down to New Mexico to see you? I know he likes you," Hayley added with childlike certainty. "He doesn't ever talk to any woman the way he talks to you."

He might like her, Dallas thought dismally, but not enough to warrant a trip to New Mexico. And neither of them were really cut out for a long-term, long-distance relationship—and Dallas didn't think she'd survive a fling with Boone. It was already going to be hard to say goodbye....

Dallas tried to clear the knot of emotions in her throat. "Well, it would be nice if the two of you came down for a visit. I'd like that," she added huskily.

The sound of a vehicle suddenly caught Hayley's attention and she looked around Dallas's shoulder. "Oh, there's Dad now! I'll talk to you later, Dallas!"

Dallas turned to see the girl climb over the corral fence and race to where Boone was getting out of the old work truck. He spotted Hayley almost immediately and waited at the side of the vehicle until she reached him.

Even though she was fifty yards away and couldn't hear a word being said, Dallas felt as though she was eavesdropping, so she turned her attention back to the horses. She'd find out soon enough if Hayley got to make the trip with her friend.

A few minutes later, she was smoothing a hand over the rump of the brown mare, when Boone's voice suddenly sounded behind her.

"Do the horses still look okay to you?"

Her heart tripping rapidly in her chest, she turned to face him. He looked a bit tired, but other than that there was nothing in his expression that said he was thinking about last night and the way they'd parted.

"They look good," she said. "I just thought I'd have a little visit with them this morning. And tell them about the long trip they have ahead of them."

"You might hope they didn't understand. The most any of these have traveled in a horse trailer is about a hundred miles. That's when I picked them up at auction."

She looked away from him and over to the opposite

end of the corral, where the horses were milling around
a hay manger. "I'll make sure I make plenty of stops to
let them rest. And I've brought a water barrel so that I
can take this water they're accustomed to back with me
for the trip. Horses rarely like to drink when they're on
the road. Especially if the water is different."

"Good thinking."

Jamming her hands into the pocket of her coat, she
turned her attention back to him. "Thanks. I try to be
prepared. I just wasn't prepared for a truck breakdown.
But…things happen for a reason."

He lifted his gaze away from her to stare off at the distant mountains. "I suppose Hayley talked to you about
going to Vegas?"

"Yes."

"I gave her permission to go. But it wasn't until afterward that I realized I should've consulted you first."

"Me? Whatever for? She's your daughter."

He turned his gaze back to her and this time she could
see all sorts of emotion traipsing across his face. "Yes.
But you might not…feel comfortable staying here at the
ranch with just the two of us. If you don't, I'll take you
into town to the hotel."

He was giving her a chance to escape. From this place,
from him and all the heated attraction that flared between them. But now that she'd been given the chance,
she realized she didn't want to run from it all. She wanted
to stay right here with him.

Oh, God, what did that mean? she wondered. That
she'd already fallen in love with the man?

Seeing he was waiting for a response from her, she
said, "That won't be necessary. I'm a grown woman. I
certainly don't need a twelve-year-old chaperone to make
me feel comfortable with you."

His nostrils flared as he drew in a deep breath and for a moment she thought she saw a flicker of surprise in his eyes. "I'm glad you feel that way."

"Actually, I'm surprised that you're letting Hayley go. She's not talked to me that much about going places. And without you going along on the trip...well, I was expecting you to give her a resounding no."

Humor suddenly slanted his lips and as always, she was surprised at how different he looked when he smiled or laughed. The man deserved to be happy, she thought. And oh, how she wished she could be the woman to make him that way. But their lives were so mismatched that she'd be crazy to let herself think they could ever merge them together. Last night he'd made it pretty plain that he wouldn't give up this ranch for anything or anyone. So that meant if Dallas ever wanted a relationship with the man, she'd have to do all the giving. Could she be happy with that?

The answer is inconsequential, Dallas, because Boone isn't going to ask you to give up anything. Not for him. You've kissed the man a few times and you've felt something growing between you. But it isn't love he's looking for.

"I'm friends of the Harrisons—the family she'll be going with," he explained. "I trust them to take good care of Hayley. And this is a nice opportunity for her. Since Mick is the only hired hand I have, I don't have many chances to take my daughter on trips away from the ranch. It puts too much of a load on Mick. So I want to give her this chance to go out and enjoy herself. Especially since it's Christmastime."

Dallas shot him a broad smile. "So there is a bit of Santa Claus in you, after all," she teased. "I thought if I kept looking I might find it."

A sheepish grin touched his face. "I guess I do come off as a bit of a Scrooge. But I'm not totally heartless."

Her expression sobered as she looked up at him. "No. I never thought you were."

He awkwardly cleared his throat. "Well, I've got things to do."

She nodded. "I'll go see if I can help Hayley gather her things for the trip. Will you be taking her into town to meet your friends?"

"No. Mick will be driving out about lunchtime. He'll drop her by the Harrisons'."

"I see. Okay. I'll, uh…see you later then," she told him. And then what? she thought, as she watched him walk away. What would the two of them do tonight? Sit in the family room and stare at each other? Oh, Lord, she couldn't think about that now. She couldn't think about it at all.

A little before noon, Dallas and Boone stood in the driveway and waved goodbye to Hayley as she climbed into Mick's truck and the ranch hand drove away.

"Cash, clothes and a credit card. I think she has everything she needs to get by for tonight and tomorrow. If not, the Harrisons will take care of it," Boone said as he continued to watch Mick's black Ford travel across the dusty desert floor.

As Dallas's gaze followed his example, she was amazed at how touched she was to see the girl leave. Before she'd climbed into Mick's truck, Hayley had given her father a tight hug and then she'd flung her arms around Dallas and hugged her close. And for a brief moment Dallas had felt like a real mother.

Now, as the black truck disappeared behind a distant

hill, she had to face the fact that she might never see Hayley again.

"She'll be fine," Dallas said around the lump in her throat. "And maybe she'll be back before I leave for New Mexico."

He darted a strange look at her. "Is seeing Hayley again that important to you?"

Directing her gaze to the ground, she blinked at the hot mist threatening to cloud her vision. "Don't get me wrong, Boone, my days are spent with children. Many of whom I've grown really attached to. But Hayley—there's something about her that makes me want to protect her. Love her."

Suddenly his arm came around her shoulder and its comforting weight told her that he understood.

"C'mon, let's go in the house for a minute. I want to talk to you about something."

The minute they stepped through the back door and into the kitchen, Dallas turned on him.

"What? Is something wrong?"

With a comical frown, he shook his head. "No. Why? Are you anticipating trouble?"

She blushed. "Sorry. I guess I'm...just feeling antsy. Christmas is nearly here and my family keeps calling, reminding me that I don't have much time to make the drive back home. I've never spent the holiday away from the ranch." She let out a nervous laugh. "I guess they think the place will fall apart without me."

"They're missing you. That's all. But I expect Marti to call tomorrow and say your truck is ready to go. That's why, with Hayley gone, I thought it might be a good time for you and I to take a little trip of our own this afternoon."

She stared at him. "A trip? Where?"

He chuckled. "From the look on your face you're thinking it must be the end of the earth. But I promise it's only a couple of hours from here. Mustangs run in a certain area near the mountains. I thought you might enjoy seeing a herd of them in the wild."

It was all she could do to keep from flinging her arms around him. "Oh, Boone! I would love it! But your work—I don't want to put you behind."

He shook his head. "I don't think a few hours away from this place will cause it to go to ruination. And like you said—it is nearly Christmas. I'd like a treat myself."

"So when do we leave?" she asked excitedly.

"As soon as you can be ready."

"Give me five minutes," she said and raced out of the room.

Ten minutes later, the two of them drove away from the ranch house with a backpack loaded with a thermos of coffee, a bag full of snacks and Dallas's digital camera. Once they reached the main highway, Boone turned north toward the distant range of mountains.

When he'd said the trip took two hours, she'd expected that time to be mostly highway travel. But they'd traveled less than an hour when he turned west onto a graveled road that wound through scrubby desert hill country. Eventually, the hills grew steeper and the juniper and pinyon became thicker, while sage grew tall along the rocky slopes.

When the road finally narrowed down to little more than a rough trail, Boone pulled the truck to the side and parked.

"We'll have to hoof it from here if we expect to see anything. If the horses do happen to be close by, they'll most likely be grazing on the other side of this ridge. There's a creek over there and shelter from the wind."

Dallas reached for her sock cap and gloves as Boone climbed to the ground and shouldered on the backpack. Moments later, they left the locked truck and skirted along the base of a rocky bluff until they spotted a path open enough to climb.

"I'll take it slow," Boone told her as they started upward through the scrubby pine. "Just stay behind me and watch your step. The ground is usually loose."

The higher they climbed the windier it became. By the time they reached the crest of the butte, the north wind was whipping the evergreens and bending the sage. But thankfully the sun was bright and Dallas didn't feel a bit cold, even though she could tell her cheeks were reddened by the wind.

"This is a fantastic view!" Dallas exclaimed as the two of them walked closer to the west rim of the bluff and peered out at the valley floor sweeping off in all directions. She pointed to a certain spot several miles in the distance. "Is that the river? That green ribbon way off there?" she asked.

"That's one of them. But that's not the creek where we're going. It's in a canyon directly below us."

Dallas tried to peer below them, but all she could see was a steep cliff covered with rock and more gnarled juniper. "Won't the horses smell us or hear us coming?"

"With any luck we might be downwind of them. And the wind might help muffle the sounds of our movements." He looked at her and shrugged. "And there's a chance the mustangs might not even be in this area today."

She smiled at him, then turned her gaze back to the valley floor. "It doesn't matter if we miss seeing the horses. This sight alone was worth the drive." *And getting to spend the time with you,* she wanted to add, then bit her tongue on the thought. What would he think, how would he react if she said such a thing to him? She desperately wanted to find out. But he'd more or less walked away from her last night and she didn't want to risk ruining this outing with another rejection.

"I'm glad you like it," he said gently, then with a hand on her arm, urged her forward. "C'mon, let's go partway down the bluff and see if we can pick up any signs that the horses have been here."

The descent was practically vertical and much tougher going than the climb. Several times Dallas slipped and slid, but managed to grab hold of rock and sage to prevent herself from tumbling forward. Ahead of her, Boone was having his own problems staying upright and the most he could do was glance over his shoulder every few minutes to make sure she was keeping up.

"There should be a little plateau not far from here," he finally called back to her. "We'll stop there."

"I'll be ready!"

Traveling in switchback fashion, they descended about twenty more yards before the plateau came into view. Boone reached the piece of flat ground first, then just as Dallas was making the final descent to join him, her boot hit a loose rock and she fell backward. Landing on her butt, she slipped and skidded several feet before a protrusion of rock finally stopped her.

Rushing to her side, Boone knelt over her. "Dallas! Are you hurt?"

Smothering a laugh, she reached for his hand. "Only my pride. And I probably made so much noise I've scared away every living thing within a mile of here."

"I doubt it. Besides, we're not worried about that. Are you sure you didn't hurt something?"

The concern in his eyes made her feel very special

and for one split second she considered slipping a hand around the back of his neck and pulling his face down to hers. The idea left her more winded than the fall and she shook her head to try to push away the longing.

"I'm fine. Really. Just help me up and we'll move on."

He pulled her to her feet and she quickly began to swat the dirt and twigs from the rump of her jeans.

He brushed bits of gravel and debris from the back of her coat. "If it makes you feel any better I spotted tracks on the plateau. The horses have been up this way fairly recently."

"Are you sure it wasn't mountain goats? I can't imagine a horse up here," she joked.

He chuckled lowly, but it was the warm light in his brown eyes that tugged at her.

"They're a bit more agile than you are." He took a tight hold on her hand. "Let's go have a look at the creek."

The shelf in the side of the bluff was no more than four feet wide at most, and the drop over the edge would be a deadly one for man or beast. Thankfully, Dallas wasn't squeamish about heights. Still, the grip of Boone's fingers was comforting as they moved over the flat but narrow ground.

Eventually, they came upon a break in the bluff that gave them a nice view of a brushy narrow canyon with a creek tumbling over boulders and beds of river rock. Boone found a bent juniper that shielded them from the wind and they sat together on the twisted trunk.

"The canyon makes a natural shelter from the cold and even in the winter like this, there's usually some sort of vegetation here for them to graze on," Boone explained. "If we're lucky we'll see them."

"How in the world did you find this place? It's in the middle of nowhere."

He removed the backpack and laid it carefully to one side. "We're on BLM land here. Before we got here we passed through National Forest. I used to have a friend that worked as a ranger for this area and he told me where to find the horses. That was years ago. And thank God, it hasn't changed."

She reached over and laid her hand on his arm. "This was so thoughtful of you to go to the trouble of bringing me up here, Boone. Thank you."

His lips took on a sheepish slant. "I don't think most women would have enjoyed the trek. But...you're different. So I took a chance."

Their faces were only inches apart and as her eyes scanned his rugged features, her heart beat fast. "You mean I'm not your typical woman," she stated wryly. "The delicate, feminine type."

His eyes softened as they roamed from her face to her feet and back again. "What are you talking about? Everything about you spells woman to me."

"Thank you," she said softly.

He shook his head. "Did someone ever lead you to believe you were lacking in the woman department?"

She looked away from him and down toward the creek. The sun was sparkling upon the water like diamonds and her lips curved to a mocking smile as she thought about the huge diamond engagement ring Allen had once slid onto her finger. The gem had been real, but he'd been a phony. Still, it had crushed her self-esteem when he'd run straight to his old flame's arms. No woman wanted to be cast aside for another.

"Not exactly. But I—" She looked at him and suddenly it all came pouring out of her. "The man I was engaged to threw me over at the last minute for another woman. That pretty much squashed the image I had of myself."

Boone's eyes narrowed as he studied her face. "Is this for real? Your fiancé left you?"

She supposed she should have been embarrassed to admit such a thing to this man. But she wasn't. He'd experienced enough heartache to understand. "It's true. The wedding was only two weeks away and it was going to be a big affair. Food, flowers, the church, my dress, a band for the reception—everything was already set and then Allen tells me he can't go through with it."

"I suppose he had a good reason," he said grimly.

"Oh, yes. His conscience. He confessed that he'd only planned to marry me to get into the Donovan money. He'd believed living a rich lifestyle would be enough to make him happy. But I guess the thought of being *that* close to me for the rest of his life cooled his heels. He ended our engagement and went back to his old girlfriend—the one before he wooed me," she added sarcastically. "She was the delicate, feminine sort."

"I'll bet she couldn't hike a mountain or ride a horse like you do," he said lowly. "And I'll bet her hair didn't shine like a copper penny and her lips didn't taste like a sweet dream."

With each word he spoke, his face grew nearer and Dallas's heart beat faster.

"You don't have to feed my ego, Boone. I've been over Allen for a long time. In fact, now that I look back on it I don't think I ever truly loved him. I was in love with the idea of having a husband. So he saved us both some misery."

"But the ordeal hurt you."

She breathed deeply as his lips hovered near hers. "Terribly," she admitted. "I still don't trust myself with men."

"Why?"

"Because. Apparently I don't have enough sense to know a bad one when I see one."

His hand came up to touch her cheek. "How do you see me?"

"Dangerous."

"Why?" he asked.

"Because I want you," she said simply.

"And that's bad?"

Her sigh was lost in the wind. "Like I said last night, there's a thousand miles between us. That's real bad."

Slowly, he eased his head back from hers and the fact that he was pulling away filled Dallas with disappointment.

"Last night, after you left the family room, I felt awful. I felt like a selfish bastard because I—" He broke off and his gaze was full of agony as he looked at her. "The ranch—"

"You don't have to explain, Boone," she said softly. "I understand the deep love you have for it. It's your home, the anchor you've always had in your life."

"Yes, it's always been that. But it's also been an albatross of sorts."

Surprised that he would say such a thing, she looked at him. "What do you mean? Because of your father and the rift it caused between you?"

He looked away from her and down at the creek and when Dallas saw him swallow, she knew he was about to let loose a part of him that he never allowed anyone to know or see.

"Partly. But it ruined my marriage. It caused me to lose a wife and Hayley to lose her mother."

"How so?"

He glanced at her from the corner of his eye. "You just talked about not being the delicate, feminine sort...well, my ex-wife Joan was exactly that. She was a meek little thing that was so timid she was afraid to pet the ranch dogs, much less get close to the horses."

Dallas's brows shot up with disbelief. "Dear God, Boone, how did you ever get hooked up with that sort? Allen was a lying bastard, but he was at least compatible in other ways."

He wiped a hand over his face. "It's easy to fall for someone, Dallas, when you're lonely down to your very gut. I'd lost my grandparents and then gone through the struggles with my father. The few women I had dated never turned into anything serious. Because of the ranch, I think. None of them wanted to live the isolated life and I could hardly blame them. But Joan—well, she was different. She came from a broken family like me. Her folks had considered her to be just another mouth to feed and they sent her to live with her aunt and uncle in Pioche. That's where I met her. She was making plans to work her way through college, but that all changed once we decided to get married. She was thrilled at the idea of having a real home and I was only too happy to give her one."

"But it didn't work," Dallas said solemnly.

The shake of his head was barely discernable. "Nothing worked. She couldn't stand the isolation, the animals, the long hours I had to devote to working it. I could only take her to town so much, but she wasn't satisfied. Then the fighting started. She wanted me to sell out and give my father his part of the money."

Dallas was incredulous. "Did she believe that Newt deserved money?"

Boone's lips twisted to a grim line. "At that time he was still making noises about his part of the estate and

Joan used Newt's demands as extra leverage to get what she wanted—for us to move to civilization."

"Obviously, you refused."

"I was already having serious doubts about Joan's mental stability and our marriage. I didn't want to make the mistake of losing my home, too. But then Joan told me she was pregnant and I hoped beyond hope that a child would bring contentment and purpose to her life. I thought the baby was just what she needed. But the pregnancy was a difficult one. She spent the last few weeks in bed."

"Oh. That couldn't have helped matters."

"No. And once she had the baby, something happened to ruin any chances of her having another."

Hayley had hinted as much, Dallas thought. "I guess she was bitter about that, too."

"No. She was glad. She had no interest in being a mother to Hayley or any future baby. Oh, she tried. And she pretended to care, but after a while she wasn't fooling anyone. She ignored Hayley and fell into a deep depression. Finally, she had to be admitted to a mental hospital up in Ely and she stayed there several months before she finally faced up to the fact that she wasn't cut out to be a wife or mother and she especially wasn't cut out to live on a ranch in the middle of nowhere."

Her heart aching for him, she reached for his hand. "Oh, Boone. I'm so sorry. For you and for Hayley. And I—" She shook her head with confusion. "I can't understand how the woman can ignore her own daughter."

"Neither could I at first. Until the doctors explained that Joan lacks that thing inside of us humans that gives us the ability to bond with our offspring and other people. All of Joan's thoughts are centered on herself. She's incapable of loving others."

"But Hayley says she's remarried."

"That's true. But believe me, it's not a love connection. She's simply in the marriage for convenience and financial security." He squeezed her hand. "So you see, you're not the only one who misjudged. I made a whopping mistake when I married Joan."

"Is that why you don't want to marry again?" Dallas dared to ask.

His brown eyes filled with shadows. "Wouldn't you be afraid to try again?"

She swallowed as emotions swelled in her chest. "I was for a long time. But I—I don't want to live the rest of my life alone, Boone. I want children. I want a man to love me. Really love me."

With a groan of anguish he turned to her. "Dallas. Dallas. I wish—I wish I could be that man."

His hands cupped the sides of her face and she closed her eyes as emotions flooded through her. "You could be that man, Boone. If you wanted to be."

He didn't say anything and then suddenly his mouth came down on hers in a hungry, savage kiss that shot her senses straight up to the sky.

Instantly her arms wrapped around his neck, her lips opened to his. She didn't know what it was that made her long for this man; she only knew that once she was in his arms, once his lips were moving over hers, she felt whole and right.

"Boone." She whispered his name as their lips parted and he buried his face against the side of her neck. "I wish things could be different. That there were no miles, or past, or anything between us."

He moved his lips back to her cheek, where his breath warmed her, tempted her with another kiss. "Let's not

think about that now. This day is just for being together—
for pleasure. Not worries."

He was right. She didn't want to think about tomorrow or what it might bring. She simply wanted to focus on the present and the joy of being with this man.

"Yes," she murmured. "Let's just think about right now. And each other."

"Dallas."

Her name was all he said before his lips returned to hers. And Dallas gladly gave herself up to his kiss.

Chapter Ten

The ground was cold and the wind was even cooler, but Dallas felt nothing but heat as Boone eased her off the juniper trunk and onto the ground next to it.

With her arms still wrapped firmly around him, he ravaged her face and lips with kisses while his hands pushed off her cap and stabbed into the thick waves of her fiery hair.

She wanted him. Every part of him. Over and over the chant raced through her mind until she could think of nothing but being next to him, touching him, tasting him. And when she felt his hands dip beneath her sweater and slide wantonly up to her breasts, she moaned with sheer pleasure.

As his lips feasted upon hers, his thumb and forefingers kneaded her nipples and his hips aligned with hers. Beneath the fly of his jeans, she could feel the bulge of his manhood straining against the denim and her feminine core ached to receive that part of him.

Desperately, she parted his coat and drove her hands beneath the tails of his shirt. His skin was hot and smooth, the muscles like iron bands wrapped tightly around his torso. Her fingers searched each slope and bump across his back, then rounded each side of his waist to meet at his navel.

Her hands were inching lower and lower to the button on the band of his jeans, when suddenly a horse's loud whinny echoed down the canyon and then another quickly returned the call.

Boone's head jerked up as he listened intently to the soft neighs sounding just below them. "Oh, hell! The mustangs are here," he whispered.

A part of Dallas wanted to jerk him back down to her, to tell him to forget about the horses and make love to her. But the arrival of the wild mustangs could hardly be ignored by either of them and she realized their heated moment had ended, at least for now.

"Then we…uh, better go see," she told him, careful to keep her voice low.

His lips slanted to a rueful grin. "Yeah, we'd better. That's what we came here for."

Rising stealthily to his feet, he gave her a hand up, then motioned for her to remain in a crouched position as together they moved forward to the rim of the shelf.

As soon as they were near enough to peer straight down into the canyon, Dallas had to slap a hand over her mouth to stifle a gasp. The picture before her was too beautiful for words and she could only stare in wonder at the wild horses splashing through the creek and milling along the sloped banks. The group of animals consisted of all ages, colors and sizes, with most of them sporting extremely long manes and shaggy forelocks, a condition that emphasized their wild image even more.

The touch of Boone's hand on hers suddenly caught her attention and she looked over to see him silently pointing down the draw to a bay mare with a weanling-aged colt at her side. The colt was trying his best to nurse, but the mother persistently nudged him along, toward the rest of the herd.

Smiling, Dallas mouthed, "He's hungry."

"He's stubborn," Boone replied.

"Typical man," Dallas whispered.

Grinning at her remark, he leaned over and whispered in her ear, "We men know what we want and when we want it."

She shot him a saucy look, but he didn't make a move to kiss her. Instead, he eased into a sitting position on the ground, then drew her into the circle of his arms, so that her back was comfortably resting against his chest.

They sat that way for more than a half hour, silently watching the meandering horses and pointing occasionally to the frolicking babies. But eventually, a rangy red stallion moved the herd on down the canyon and out of sight.

When the last horse finally disappeared behind a bend in the creek, Boone pushed to his feet and helped Dallas to hers.

"We'd better be going," he said. "We need to be out of the mountains by sundown."

She agreed and they headed back over the same trail they'd taken earlier. On this side of the bluff the climb out was even steeper, and several times Boone reached to give her a helping hand as they maneuvered over slippery rocks and around tall, thick bushes of sage.

By the time they reached the truck, Dallas was feeling the exertion of the trek, but the joy of the afternoon made her forget her weary muscles. And the pleasure coursing through her veins was only partly due to the mustang sightings.

Something had happened between her and Boone while they'd been up there on the bluff. She'd shared things with him that she'd never shared with any man. And she was fairly certain his troubled past with Joan was not something he discussed with anyone, much less another woman. If the horses hadn't arrived at that moment, the two of them would have made love right there on the cold ground. The reality of that had been apparent to both of them. And now, though neither had spoken it in words, when they looked at each other, it was like they both understood and accepted the fact that they could no longer deny the desire that burned between them.

The ride back to the ranch was passed with general conversation about the horses and other shared interests. Neither mentioned the night ahead. Or that the two of them would be entirely alone. But Dallas was thinking about it. And she knew Boone was, too.

When they finally reached the ranch house night had fallen and so had the temperature. Boone let Dallas out at the back fence, then drove on to the barns so that he could tend to the nightly feeding chores.

Inside, Dallas quickly changed out of her dirty clothes, then went to the kitchen to find something for their supper. By the time Boone returned to the house, she was putting canned soup and fried bologna sandwiches on the table.

His brows arched with surprise as he glanced at her handiwork. "You didn't have to fix anything."

Feeling ridiculously nervous, she gestured toward

the food on the table. "It's nothing. Just soup and sand-wiches."

Dear Lord, her voice sounded as breathless as if she'd just run a mile.

He went over to the sink, washed his hands, then dried them on a paper towel. As he walked back over to her, she could feel her heart thumping hard against her breast-bone. Something on his face said his mind was hardly on food.

"We'll eat it later," he murmured.

As soon as she nodded, he reached for her hand and led her out of the kitchen and straight to his bedroom.

It was the only room in the house that she'd not seen before, and as they stepped inside the dimly lit space, she only managed to catch glimpses of dark wood furniture and a queen-size bed covered with a plain brown com-forter, before he tugged her into his arms and planted a long, searching kiss on her lips.

"I've thought of you in my arms—like this—so many times," he murmured, his nose nuzzling the shell of her ear. "If you think it's wrong, tell me. Tell me now."

She tightened the hold she had on his waist. "I wouldn't be here if I thought it was a mistake," she told him, her voice vibrating with raw emotion.

He sighed and then, with a hand at the back of her head, he tilted her face up to his. "I can't make prom-ises," he said in a choked voice. "Promises that I can't keep. That wouldn't be right or fair."

With one hand she reached up and tenderly stroked her fingers along his cheekbone. "I'm not asking for prom-ises, Boone. Just love me. Right now. That's all I ask."

Satisfied with her reply, he lifted her into his arms and gently placed her in the middle of the bed.

Dallas promptly looked down at her feet and giggled. "Boone! My boots!"

Laughing, he joined her on the bed. "Don't worry, my little darlin', those will be off soon enough. Along with everything else."

He made good on his word. In less than three minutes' time her boots and clothes were tossed to a pile in the floor and his were lying in a messy heap next to them.

After that, Boone couldn't touch her enough or look at her enough to satisfy his senses. She was like a sweet dessert, all white and soft and full of decadent sugar. He didn't know whether to lap every inch of her with his tongue or to simply let his hands do all the searching. Either way, just having her naked curves next to his was pulsing hot blood to every point in his body.

With his lips against hers, he said, "I've been fighting like hell against this. But ever since I kissed you that first night after you arrived, I've been crazy to have you close—to make love to you."

"Oh, Boone, I don't know what you do to me—but I can't think straight whenever you touch me. I don't want to think at all," she admitted.

Her hands were making a slow foray down his chest and across his belly and he couldn't stop a needy groan from rolling past his lips. "All I can think is that I'm damned glad that truck of yours refused to start. Otherwise, this wouldn't have happened and I wouldn't have known the heaven of having you in my bed."

"All things happen for a reason," she whispered.

And the reason is you, he wanted to add, but the words stuck in his throat as she chose that moment to pull his head down to hers.

After that, words were unnecessary as he used his lips and hands to show her how very much he wanted and needed her. And in the matter of a few short moments, their arms and legs were tangled, the fire between them flaming high enough to scorch the bedcovers.

It had been ages since Boone had been with a woman and he told himself that the need for sexual release was the reason his hands were trembling and his heart pounding like a drum in his chest. It had nothing to do with the way her dreamy eyes smiled up at him, the way her lips gave and gave and then gave more, or the way her hands held on to him as though she never wanted to let go. No, he thought desperately. She was simply a woman and he was in need of a warm, willing body.

That's what he told himself. But deep down he knew all of that was a lie. Because he was afraid to admit how much she was shaking him, pushing him to the edge, turning his heart into a warm pool of love.

Beneath him, he could feel her body arching toward his, silently begging for release, and with his mouth on hers, he parted her thighs with his knee.

"Dallas—darling—are you...protected?" he asked, his words strangled with desire.

"Don't worry. I'm on the pill," she assured him.

Relief rushed through him, yet even if she'd said she wasn't on birth control, he doubted he could've stopped himself from accepting all that she was ready to give. Desire was pushing all rational thought from his head.

"That's good, baby. Because I can't wait to have you."

Her answer was to plant her hands against his buttocks and draw his hips down to hers.

All too willing to please her, Boone positioned himself and with one long, slow thrust entered her moist folds. Exquisite warmth suddenly enveloped him, surrounded him with a pleasure so intense it momentarily robbed his breath. But the moment she arched upward, the push drew him even deeper into her body, forcing him to gasp and suck in the oxygen his lungs were screaming for.

After that everything turned into a flurry of movement as they began to move together, each frantically straining to be closer. Dallas's hands were all over him, tempting, coaxing, pushing him to give her more and more of himself, while his own hands couldn't get enough of her smooth skin, the soft mounds of her breasts, the long sinewy muscles of legs, the flare of her hips.

Faster and faster, the rhythm of their bodies raced toward that place they both so desperately needed. Yet Boone didn't want to go there. Not yet. He wasn't ready for this taste of heaven to end. And even with desire gripping his mind, he realized he would be losing more than just physical pleasure. Moment by moment he could feel his heart cracking, slipping away bit by bit as it poured from him and straight into her.

He couldn't let it go. If he did there would be nothing left to him. Yet when he felt himself reach the edge, he couldn't stop himself from plunging into the deep, hot pool of her love.

"Boone! Boone!"

He heard her cry his name, but then the roar of throbbing blood filled his ears and he heard nothing else as he desperately drove into her. Over and over. Until the final release came and his body collapsed over hers.

The weight of Boone's lax body was heavy against her laboring lungs, but Dallas didn't care. She welcomed the load, relished the feel of his hot sweaty skin melded to hers.

Pressed together, their bodies still connected, they felt as one to Dallas and she desperately wanted to hold on to the intimate moment for as long as she could. Because it wouldn't last. It couldn't last.

The sad thought had hardly formed in her mind when he rolled off her. Yet his hand remained on her waist as he stretched himself close to her side and nuzzled his nose in the hair near her temple.

"I hope I didn't squash you," he murmured.

Rolling toward him, she wrapped an arm around his waist. "You didn't."

"If I was too rough I—"

Her fingers touched his lips before he could finish the rest of his sentence. "Everything was right," she murmured huskily. "So very right."

He released a long breath, then placed a gentle kiss on her temple. Dallas closed her eyes and marveled at the warm, sweet contentment flowing through her body. She'd only known Boone a few short days and yet she'd made love to him as though they'd been partners for years, as though it was completely proper to give herself to him with such wild abandon.

"Dallas, there's something I think I should say. About Hayley. And tonight."

Tilting her head back, she looked at him. "What about Hayley?"

The corners of his mouth turned downward. "I just wanted to explain that I didn't allow her to go on the shopping trip just to... Just so that this could happen. When I gave her permission, this thing with you and me wasn't in my mind."

A lazy smile tilted her lips. "The thought never occurred to me. You allowed Hayley to go on the trip because you thought it would be good for her—a treat for her." Still smiling, she pressed her cheek against his chest. "Boone, there's nothing manipulative about you. Like I said before, things happen for a reason. Besides, even if you had planned all this, I think I would have willingly fallen into your trap anyway."

"Traps are for rats. And you're not a rat. You're an angel," he said huskily as his fingertips slipped lazily across her shoulder and down her back. "A Christmas angel sent straight to me."

Christmas. Her family would be gathered around the giant tree that was erected every year in the family room. Grandmother Kate would play the piano and carols would be sung. Gifts would be exchanged and with spirits high, everyone would be laughing and celebrating Christ's birth. The beautiful image was a tradition she could always count on at her home on the Diamond D. But Christmas would be something entirely different for Boone and Hayley, she thought sadly. The rooms in their house wouldn't be filled with family. There would be no rowdy laughter or piles of decadent food.

That night her truck had failed to start, all she'd been able to think about was getting her business done and getting back home for the holiday. But now, though she would miss her family terribly, she realized that she didn't want to leave this man or his daughter. She wanted to give them all the joy that she could. Because she loved them. Oh, yes. She loved them. But would Boone want her love? Right now she dared not ask. Right now, she wanted him to get use to having her in his arms. And later, God willing, he would realize that he wanted to keep her there for all time.

"You've gone quiet on me, Dallas. Is something wrong?"

She moved her head just enough to let her gaze meet his. "No," she hedged. "I was just thinking…about things. This trip has turned out to be—well, I never expected anything like this to happen. When I spoke to you over the phone, before I left the Diamond D, I thought I was speaking with a much older man," she admitted. "I thought I was going to come up here and meet a gray-headed gentleman with a kindly wife and a few grand-kids underfoot."

He chuckled. "And I thought you were going to be one of those rough, rawboned women that had never worn a dress in her life and her main goal was saving the earth from human destruction."

She laughed at his description and the lighthearted moment was just the thing she needed to push thoughts of tomorrow out of her head. "Little did we know."

Resting his forehead against hers, he said, "This af-ternoon, when we watched the mustangs together, I just want you to know that I— That place—I've not shared it with anyone else."

It was his way of saying she was special to him and for now that was enough to bring joy to her heart.

Slipping her arm around his neck, she brought her lips next to his. "And I'll never forget that you took me there, Boone. Never."

The next morning, long before daylight, Dallas roused from her sleep to see Boone standing by the bed, button-ing his shirt.

Rising up on her elbow, she asked groggily, "Is it time to get up?"

Quickly he leaned over her and with a hand on her shoulder urged her back against the mattress. "It's still very early. Go back to sleep, darling."

She started to protest, but he kissed her cheek and pulled the covers back over her shoulders. Too tired to argue, she closed her eyes and was sound asleep before he ever left the room.

It was much later before she finally woke a second

time and after taking a quick shower in her own bedroom, she dressed in jeans and a black sweater and left for the kitchen.

Boone was nowhere in sight and the coffee was burned black from sitting too long on the warmer. She was waiting for a fresh pot to finish dripping when the phone at the end of the counter rang.

A quick glance at the caller ID identified her mother's cell number and Dallas quickly snatched up the receiver.

"Mom! Hello!"

"Oh. I was about to hang up. I was hoping Mr. Barnett would answer and tell me that you'd already left for home. But I can see that's not the case."

Mr. Barnett. How odd that sounded, Dallas thought. She'd just slept with the man. But thankfully her mother didn't know that. And if Fiona did learn about it, what would she think? That her daughter was a complete fool for falling into bed with a man she hardly knew?

But she did know Boone, her heart argued. And she could no longer deny the fact that she loved him. Somehow these past few days her feelings had grown from physical attraction to a heart-deep bond.

"Not yet. From what the mechanic has told me, I'm expecting him to have the truck ready to go sometime today. If it's past noon before I hear from him, then I won't have time to leave today. The trip in to Pioche then back out here to pick up the horses will take at least three hours and I don't want to start driving to New Mexico at night," she explained.

Fiona sighed. "Your father and I wouldn't want you to do that. So at the latest you believe you'll be starting home tomorrow?" she asked in a hopeful voice.

Dallas squeezed her eyes shut as her torn emotions tugged her in all directions. "Yes. I suppose so."

There was a moment's pause and then Fiona said, "Is anything wrong, Dallas? You don't exactly sound excited about coming home. Have you forgotten it's nearly Christmas? You've already missed so many parties! And everyone is asking about you—missing you!"

Her throat was so tight she had to clear it before she could speak. "I haven't forgotten, Mom. It's just that things have been happening up here. And—"

"Are you enjoying yourself?" Fiona interrupted.

Was she? Dallas asked herself. Boone and Hayley had brought so much joy to her life. The sort of joy she'd never experienced before. She felt as though she'd become a part of their family. But as far as she knew those feeling were all one-sided. Boone had made love to her, but he'd hardly said that he loved her. There was a world of difference.

"Yes. I am," Dallas finally admitted. "Boone is— I've come to...like him very much. And his daughter is so cute and special."

Several seconds of silence passed and Dallas knew Fiona was carefully weighing every word she'd spoken. Instead of being thirty-two years old she felt more like seventeen and desperately in need of her mother's approval.

"I see."

"Do you really, Mom?"

"You've fallen in love with the man. I can hear it in your voice."

Dallas tried to laugh but only succeeded in making a choking noise. "I never could hide anything from you."

Fiona sighed. "That's true, Dallas. You've always been as transparent as a piece of Scotch tape. But you've also been a wise girl. If you believe this man is worthy of your love, he must be very special."

Dallas groaned. "Are you forgetting about Allen? Getting engaged to that bastard was really a wise move on my part," she said with sarcasm.

"We're all entitled to one mistake," Fiona pointed out. "And Allen had the whole family fooled. Not just you."

And now Dallas had probably made two mistakes, she thought, then just as quickly tried to shake the dismal notion away. Loving Boone was not a mistake. Somehow they had to mesh their lives together. Otherwise she didn't think she could ever be happy without him.

"I don't know what's going to become of all this, Mom. This has all happened so quickly and—"

"Dallas, if the two of you are meant to be together it will happen, trust me."

If only she could feel that much confidence, Dallas thought. But after what Boone had gone through with Joan, she doubted he could ever trust a woman enough to allow her to be a permanent part of his life and a mother to Hayley. Obviously the two roles went hand in hand and she could never expect to be just one or the other.

"Yes. You're right," Dallas said, then added, "I'll let you know when I'll be leaving."

"You might not want to leave now," Fiona pointed out.

The biggest part of Dallas didn't want to leave. But staying wasn't an option, either. Not unless Boone asked her to.

"My family, my job, my home is on the Diamond D," she said in a low, strained voice.

"Grandmother Kate always says a woman's home is where her man is."

Closing her eyes, Dallas pressed a hand to her forehead. "That's an old-fashioned notion that went out the window about the same time suffragettes marched for a woman's right to vote," she argued. "A woman shouldn't have to be a self-sacrificing martyr just to have a man, a family."

"No. But sometimes circumstances call for a lot of giving. Maybe you need to decide just how much you love your Mr. Barnett. And then your heart will tell you how much you want to give."

Tears stung the back of Dallas's eyelids. "I need to go, Mom. I'll call you tomorrow. And tell Liam not to worry. I'll have his truck home soon."

She hung up before her mother could add anything else and quickly moved down the cabinet to pour herself a cup of coffee.

While she made herself a piece of toast and jam, she wondered if she was being a total fool to hope Boone might love her the same way that she loved him. Last night in his arms, her world had changed. She'd learned what it was like to be truly wanted, to have every inch of her body worshipped by a man.

But he'd admitted it had been a long time since he'd been with a woman in that way. Maybe she'd simply assuaged his sexual needs.

The spinning question in her head didn't stop as she swallowed down the last of her toast and left the kitchen.

Out in the ranch yard, Boone and Mick had just returned after spending more than two hours rescuing a trio of calves from a dry wash. Somehow the babies had wandered away from their mothers and climbed down into a place they didn't know how to get out of.

Now, as the two men led their mounts into the barn where they could unsaddle them out of the wind, Mick asked, "What are you going to do for Christmas?"

"Nothing."

"Nothing? What about Dallas? I'm sure she'll want to celebrate whether you do or not."

"I doubt Dallas will be here." Boone lifted the saddle from the gray's back and carried it into the tack room. As he was resting it on a wooden stand, Mick joined him in the small space. A bridle and tie-down were draped over his shoulder.

"So she's going home?"

"Was there ever any question about that?" Boone asked curtly.

Mick hung the pieces of tack on a nail, then turned to look at him. "I wasn't sure. I thought you might do something crazy and ask her to stay."

A heavy pain filled Boone's chest. "Hell, Mick. You know me better than that."

"Do I? I'm not so sure." His gaze fell to the cat rubbing against Boone's jean leg. "By the way, I've been meaning to ask where she came from."

Boone looked down at the calico. "I have no idea. She just showed up the other day."

"Showed up? That doesn't make sense. Your closest neighbor is ten miles away. She couldn't have hoofed it that far out here."

"Well, she hoofed it from somewhere. And now she's made herself at home."

"Yeah, like someone else I know."

Boone glared at him. "That was uncalled for."

Mick had the decency to look shamefaced. "Are you going to let her stay?"

Frowning, Boone bent over and stroked the cat. "Are you talking about the little calico now?"

"That's who I mean. Can't you see she's pregnant? If you let her hang around here you'll just end up having a bunch of mouths to feed."

His jaw tight, Boone looked up at his friend. "Well, what would you have me do, Mick? Get rid of her by any means? You know me better than that. Remember, I'm not Newt. I'm Boone. I happen to care about other living creatures."

"What the hell does that mean? And I'm not so sure you do care. If you cared that much you wouldn't ignore the old man the way you do."

Boone mouthed a curse. "He's a drunk, Mick. You know it. I know it. And he's never cared about anyone or anything but himself."

"I thought that honor belonged to Joan."

Fed up, Boone turned and strode out of the tack room. Mick followed on his heels with the pregnant calico trailing behind the two men.

"We've been friends for a long time, Mick, but I'll tell you right now—you're making me damned mad. I don't know what's put a burr under your collar but for the past few days you've been acting like a jerk."

"And you've been behaving like—well, not yourself," Mick answered him, then heaved out a long breath and shoved his hands into the pockets of his jeans.

Boone could see his friend was troubled, but he already had a head full of miseries. Right now, he couldn't deal with more. "I have things on my mind," Boone told him.

"Well, here's something else for you," Mick retorted. "Newt called me last night."

Boone paused in the act of slipping a nylon halter onto the gray's head. Newt rarely called anyone. What could be going on with the old man now? he wondered. "Drunk?"

"Surprisingly, he sounded sober. He wanted to know

what you were doing for Christmas. Said he'd tried to call you but you didn't answer."

"Dallas and I were gone and didn't get home until late. I checked the answering machine. He didn't bother leaving a message."

Mick shrugged. "He wants to see his granddaughter for Christmas. He says he'll be sober."

A pent-up breath eased out of Boone. "We'll see," Boone said grimly.

Relenting now, Mick walked over and placed a comforting hand on Boone's shoulder. "I know he's led a pretty sorry life, Boone. But he's lonely. And he needs you."

Mick had always been more generous-hearted and understanding toward Newt than Boone had ever been. Since the other man had been raised in a string of foster homes, Mick considered having any sort of blood parent better than none at all.

"I'll take Hayley by to see him, Mick. I always do."

Mick looked at him. "So you expect Dallas to be gone by Christmas Day?"

The question left Boone cold inside. All morning he'd tried his best not to think of Dallas leaving, of never seeing her again. After last night, it seemed impossible that something so deep and special could end so soon. But it had to end, he told himself. Dallas was a wonderful woman. He couldn't ask her to bury herself here on White River and give up everything that was dear and important to her. He'd gone down that road before and though Dallas was a much stronger person than Joan, he wasn't willing to take the chance of crushing her spirit, too.

"She'll be gone," he stated flatly. "Satisfied?"

The shuffle of Mick's footsteps sounded behind him

and he looked over his shoulder to see the other man standing only a step away. His expression was rueful, which only made Boone feel worse than terrible.

"All right, I'm sorry. I've been speaking out of line. But damn it, you're the closest thing I have to a brother. Hell, you're the closest thing I have to a relative, period. And I guess...I don't want to see you go through another nightmare like you did with Joan. I want more than that for you. And I can't see anything good for you coming out of this thing with Dallas."

Boone opened his mouth to speak, but before he could utter a word, Mick held up a pleading hand. "Wait. I'm not finished. Don't get me wrong. I like her. She's beautiful, intelligent and not afraid to get her hands dirty. She seems to know more about horses than I could ever hope to know. And on top of that she's nice. With a résumé like that, it sounds like she'd make the perfect wife for you. But you know where she's come from and it ain't a place like this."

Mick was so right it made Boone sick. "Don't worry about it, Mick. In a few days this place will go back to just you and me and Hayley. And the calico," he added pointedly. "She stays."

A faint smile twisted Mick's lips. "So Miss Holiday stays. I guess I can live with that."

But could Boone live with Dallas's leaving? That time was coming soon and the closer it got, the more his heart was beginning to break.

Live without Dallas? Oh, God, with Dallas he was just now learning to live again.

Chapter Eleven

Boone and Mick worked through lunch as they saddled up fresh mounts and rode out again, this time to move a herd of mustangs from a nearby pasture over to a fenced area with fresh grazing.

By the time this chore was finished, it was midafternoon and Boone's stomach was growling with hunger. He left Mick and his sack lunch in the barn and quickly headed to the house. But halfway there, he stopped in his tracks and stared at the truck parked near the gate of the backyard fence. While he and Mick had been away from the ranch yard, Marti had delivered Dallas's truck. And even though he'd known this time would soon arrive, it still came as a shock to him.

When he stepped into the kitchen, the radio was playing lowly, but other than that, the room was empty.

Forgetting the gnawing hunger in his belly, he quickly strode out of the room and into the family room. The lights on the Christmas tree were twinkling, but Dallas was nowhere around.

He was about to call her name, when he heard a footstep in the hall and hurried to catch up with her.

"Boone! I didn't hear you come in," she said as she paused and waited for him to join her in the dimly lit passageway.

"I just now got back." He pushed the words through his tight throat, then swallowed as his gaze searched her beautiful face. Last night he'd kissed her smooth skin and sweet lips, he'd touched the most intimate parts of her, and as incredible as it all had been, those moments and hours hadn't been nearly enough. He was certain a lifetime of loving this woman wouldn't be enough.

"Marti delivered my truck," she said solemnly. "I wasn't expecting him to go to the trouble of bringing it all the way out here."

"That's Marti. He goes beyond the call of duty to make his customers happy."

She let out a long breath. "Well, I gave him a hefty tip to show my appreciation."

"So, what now? It's a bit late in the afternoon to be leaving today, isn't it?"

She looked at him expectantly, as though she was waiting for him to say more and when he didn't, her gaze fell to the floor.

"It is rather late. By the time I got the horses loaded and everything ready to go I wouldn't have much driving time before dark. I'll just wait until morning—if it's all right with you."

Boone couldn't stand it a second longer. Latching onto her shoulders, he pulled her into his arms.

"It's more than all right with me, Dallas."

Her hands clung to him and when his lips covered

hers, the hunger he felt in her kiss literally rocked him back on his heels.

When he regained his balance he swept her up in the cradle of his arms and with her arms locked tightly around his neck, he started toward his bedroom.

Halfway there, Dallas asked, "What if Hayley comes home early?"

"She won't. It'll be tonight before she gets back. But I'll lock the door if that will ease your mind."

It would take more than locking the door to ease Dallas's mind, she thought, as he gently placed her on the bed. But she wasn't going to ruin these precious moments wrestling with that worry. This was the man she loved and she was going to enjoy loving him for as long as she could.

More than thirty minutes later, Dallas walked out of Boone's private bathroom to find him already off the bed and stuffing the tails of his shirt down in his jeans.

"I've got to get back to the barn. Mick is waiting on me to finish a bit of work we'd planned to do before he leaves for the day."

Quickly Dallas pulled on her jeans and sweater while he dealt with his boots. "I can see you're in a hurry," she said. "But I'd like to talk with you about something important."

Tugging on his boot, he raised to his full height to look at her. "Can't it wait until tonight when we'd have more time?"

She shook her head. "I'd rather do it before Hayley returns."

He walked over to her, his gaze thoughtfully studying her face. "All right. Mick will just have to wait then."

A nervous smile played with the corners of her lips. "I'm sorry. I realize this isn't a good time. But I'm not sure when a good time would be for what I want to say. I just know that our time together is running out and then it will be too late."

"Dallas, let's not—"

She touched a forefinger to his lips. "Wait, Boone. Just let me say this—I have to say it. I love you. I don't want to leave tomorrow. I don't ever want to leave you."

His brown eyes flickered with emotions she couldn't decipher. Was he glad, frustrated, uncomfortable? She was desperate to know exactly what was in this man's heart.

"Oh, Dallas, I'm honored. Never in my life have I dreamed that a woman like you would care for me. But the both of us can see it would never work for us."

"Never work? Why? Because you don't care for me?"

Groaning, he turned away from her and raked a hand through his tousled hair. As Dallas stared at the rigid line of his back, she blinked at the hot moisture stinging her eyes. Somehow she'd sensed this would be his reaction. Even so, she couldn't have left this ranch without telling him how she really felt.

"Of course I care for you!" He whirled back to her. "Do you think that last night…that what just happened with us a few minutes ago was just something physical for me?"

Hot color burned her cheeks. "I'd hoped not, but I don't know—"

His nostrils flared. "That's just it, Dallas. We don't know each other. Not enough."

She frowned. "Then how are you so certain that things couldn't work for us? We need time to—"

"We don't have time!"

"I don't have to leave tomorrow," she argued.

"Your family wants you home for Christmas. And *you* want to be home for Christmas. You need to leave in the morning. I *want* you to leave in the morning. Got that?"

His stubbornness infuriated her. "I don't *got* anything. But I can see that you've lived alone for so long that you're afraid to change! Afraid that you might see there's life beyond this ranch!"

He came to stand within an inch of her and Dallas began to outwardly tremble as she thought of all that he'd given her and all that he never would.

"This ranch is my grandparents' legacy," he said, his low voice laced with conviction. "It's everything to me."

"I'm not asking you to give it up. I would never do that."

A sad smile suddenly touched his face and Dallas's heart wanted to weep at the sight of it.

"Just like I would never ask you to give up your home and family back in New Mexico to live here. I've been through that once with another woman, Dallas. I'm not going to watch this place destroy you, too."

"I'm not Joan. And it's insulting for you to imply that I'm no better or stronger than her!"

Both his hands suddenly wrapped around her upper arms and then his cheek was pressed tightly against hers.

"My darling Dallas, please don't be angry with me. I'm not saying you're anything like her. You're strong and loving and all the special things I'd want in a woman. But you've not thought this through. You've not considered all the things you'd be giving up, sacrificing just to be here with me."

She pulled her head back far enough to look into eyes. "When I talked to my mother this morning something in my voice told her that I'd fallen in love with you. And you know what advice she gave me? She quoted my grandmother. 'A woman's home is where her man is.' The question is, Boone, are you my man?"

Anguished shadows filled his eyes. "If you're asking me if there will ever be a woman in my heart other than you—then no. But I—" He released a long, tortured breath. "You're right, Dallas, I am afraid of changing. Afraid I'll disappoint you, hurt you—see everything that's special between us break apart."

"Oh, Boone, Boone," she whispered as her hands came up to frame his face. "For a long time now I've been afraid to let myself love again. I was afraid of making another bad mistake, of choosing the wrong man, and even if he was the right one, would I be woman enough to hold on to him? But with you...I can't stop what my heart is feeling or telling me. We can make this work. If you'll just give us a chance."

Groaning with torment, he turned and walked a few feet away from her. "Go home, Dallas. Go home and think about this. And then maybe in a few months if you still want to give it a try—well, you can let me know."

She gasped. "A few months! Boone, I—"

He looked over his shoulder at her and this time his features were set like a piece of cold iron. "That's the only way I'll consider anything, Dallas. Because I'm pretty sure once you get back to New Mexico you're going to change your mind about this place—and me."

Dallas opened her mouth to argue, but instantly changed her mind. Arguing wouldn't help now. It would take more than words to convince Boone that their future was together.

"If that's the way you want it," she said quietly.

"That's the only way," he said, then strode out of the room before any more could be said.

That night Dallas was in her room packing when a knock sounded on the door.

"Dallas, I'm home! May I come in?"

"Of course," Dallas called to the girl.

The door opened and Hayley quickly rushed over to her and gave her a long hug. When she finally stepped back, she immediately noticed the open bags on Dallas's bed.

"Oh. You're getting ready to go home."

Home was here, Dallas thought. How she'd come to that conclusion she wasn't quite sure. But something had happened to her after she'd talked with her mother this morning. She'd begun looking at her life from all angles and she'd decided that in many ways she'd been living like Boone, clinging stubbornly to a piece of land as though it was the substance that made up her happiness.

Stifling a sigh, she did her best to smile brightly at the girl. "Yes. My truck is ready to go now. And my family is expecting me home for Christmas."

"Oh," Hayley said glumly. "Will you get there in time? When we were driving back from Vegas, we heard on the car radio that snow was coming. You might get into a blizzard."

Dallas had heard the same thing on the local evening news. Boone had tactfully suggested she should get an early start in order to outrun the oncoming storm. "I'll leave early enough to miss the storm. And if I drive straight through I'll be home in time to celebrate with my family."

Her head hanging now, Hayley eased down on the side of the bed. "I was hoping that you'd be here with us for Christmas. But I guess you'd rather be with your family."

I would very much like for you to be my family, Dallas wanted to say. But she couldn't put such a notion into Hayley's head. The situation was already bad enough without dragging this girl's tender heart into the mix of things.

Without thinking, Dallas picked up a shirt and stuffed

it into one of the leather bags. "What will you and your father do on that day?"

"Nothing, probably." She let out a woeful sigh. "He'll give me a Christmas card with some money in it. And I'll give him a gift. And then he'll get steaks out of the freezer and cook 'em. 'Cause that's the most special thing we eat."

Dallas studied the girl's bowed head. "You don't ever have turkey and dressing and traditional things like that?"

"We don't know how to cook that stuff."

"Oh, well, steaks are good," Dallas said with as much encouragement as she could muster. "But that's enough of that. Tell me about your trip. Did you have fun?"

For the next few minutes Hayley was happy to give Dallas a detailed description of everything she and the Harrisons had done and seen while in Las Vegas. But once she'd finished, she rose abruptly from the bed and started to the door.

"Are you leaving?" Dallas asked with surprise. "It's not bedtime yet."

"Well, I'm kinda tired. And I don't want to keep you from your packing."

Dallas glanced at the few items left lying on the bed. "You're not keeping me from packing." She walked toward the girl. "Hayley, is something wrong?"

With a broken sob, the girl ran straight to Dallas and flung her little arms tightly around her waist. "Oh, Dallas, I don't want you to go home! I want you to stay here with me and Dad—forever!"

Above Hayley's head, Dallas had to fight back her own tears. "Oh, honey, don't cry. We'll see each other again."

"We won't," she said between sobs. "You'll be just like my mom—you'll forget all about me!"

Tears slipping from her eyes, Dallas hugged the girl close. "I'll never forget you, Hayley. I promise."

Dallas had the alarm set for five o'clock the next morning, but she hadn't needed the intrusive buzzer to tell her it was time to get up. She'd hardly slept a wink as she'd spent most of the night staring at the ceiling, wondering where she was going to find the strength to drive away from Boone and Hayley.

Dressing quickly, she decided to leave her bags in the bedroom until she'd had coffee and loaded the horses. When she entered the kitchen, Boone was already at the table with a small transistor radio sitting in front of him.

The disc jockey was saying something about snow, but Dallas paid little heed as she went straight to the coffeepot and poured herself a mug. Where she lived snow was a routine thing throughout the long winter. She and her family worked through it and around it, but they never feared it.

"You can forget about leaving this morning," Boone said abruptly. "There's already a good ten inches of snow on the ground and it's still falling."

Stunned, Dallas stared at him. "Snow? Already? But I thought it wasn't supposed to be here until later tonight."

"That's what the meteorologist had predicted, but the storm front moved faster than expected."

Dallas didn't know whether to laugh or weep. "So the snow is too deep for me to drive? I have four-wheel drive," she reminded him.

He looked over his shoulder at her. "The truck would probably make it, but I can't say about a trailer loaded with six horses. I'd hate for you to put them and yourself at risk."

It would be foolish to take such a chance. Even if she

didn't wreck, just getting stuck and stranded in the snow would be dangerous, especially when she'd be traveling for miles through remote areas where there was hardly any other traffic.

She walked over to the table and sank into the chair across from his. "Well, it looks like I'll be here for Christmas, after all."

With his hands clamped around his coffee cup, he stared at the tabletop. "You'd better call your family and tell them you'll not be heading for home this morning."

"I never expected this to happen."

This brought his eyes up and with a wry expression he looked at her. "Your whole trip has been filled with the unexpected."

She swallowed hard as tears threatened to overcome her. "I spent most of the night bracing myself to tell you goodbye this morning. Now, once the snow melts, I'll have to go through it all over again."

His gaze fell back to his coffee cup. "Hayley is going to be very happy that you'll be here for Christmas."

"Is that all you have to say?"

"What do you want me to say? That the snow is a sign? Some kind of omen that says you're not supposed to leave? No, Dallas. I'm not going to let fate determine your future or mine."

Then what was going to determine it? she wanted to ask, but didn't. Tomorrow was Christmas and that was a day for miracles. Now all she could do was pray for one to come along and open Boone's heart.

Hayley was thrilled that Dallas would be staying for the holiday and the two of them decided to use the snowy day to bake cookies and whip up a batch of marshmallow fudge. As for Boone, he dressed in insulated coveralls and weatherproof boots and spent most of the day checking on the cows and calves and making sure none were caught in drifts that in some cases were waist deep.

By Christmas morning, the snow had stopped and the sun was shining in a bright blue sky. After breakfast the three of them gathered around the tree and Hayley handed out the few gifts that had been placed under the branches the night before.

Since Dallas had been snowbound and unable to drive into town for gifts, she'd had to make do with what she could find among her things. Fortunately, Fiona had dropped a new bottle of cologne into one of Dallas's bags before she'd left the Diamond D. Dallas had wrapped the soft scent for Hayley. But Boone was another matter, so she'd searched the tack room in her trailer and had discovered a brand-new saddle blanket woven of expensive mohair in deep colors of blue and green.

Hayley had loved the cologne and had drenched herself. As for Boone, he'd appeared to be genuinely touched by her gift. He'd kept rubbing his hand back and forth against the mohair and talking about how it would keep all the sweat pulled away from the horses' back.

"Open yours, Dallas," Hayley urged. "There's one from me and one from Dad."

"Okay. Let me tear into yours first," she told the girl as she unwrapped a palm-size box. "Oh! Earrings! These are beautiful, Hayley!"

The girl beamed from ear to ear. "They're real silver. And they dangle. So every time you turn your head, they'll sparkle."

"I'll love wearing them." She walked over to where Hayley was perched on the floor beside the tree, then bent down and placed a kiss on her cheek. "Thank you, sweetie. Very much."

"Now open Dad's," she urged Dallas. "I want to see what *he* got you."

Dallas cast him a furtive glance. "He shouldn't have gotten me anything."

A faint grin moved one side of his lips. "You shouldn't have gotten me anything, either."

Dallas sat back down in her chair and reached for the tiny round trinket box wrapped with printed silk fabric. She could tell that the box had been handled a great many times down through the years so it was obviously something that had meant a great deal to someone.

Her hands shook as she lifted the lid. And then as she stared down at the piece of jewelry, she momentarily forgot to breathe.

It was a cameo brooch encircled with what appeared to be real diamonds. The workmanship of the piece was exquisite and there was no doubt it would be worth a great deal of money.

"Oh, my! This is— It's absolutely beautiful!"

"What is it?" Hayley jumped from her seat on the floor and hurried over to look at the gift cradled in Dallas's hand. "It's pretty. Where did you get this, Dad?"

"It belonged to your great-grandmother," he said. "It was a special gift to her from your great-grandfather."

Lifting her head, Dallas stared at him in wonder. "I can't accept this, Boone. This piece should go to Hayley."

His gaze didn't waver from hers. "I have other things saved for Hayley. The cameo is yours now."

Dallas didn't know what to say, and even if the words had been there, she couldn't have pushed them past her burning throat.

"I… Please, excuse me," she finally choked out, then jumped to her feet and rushed from the room.

She was sitting on the side of the bed, wiping at the tears on her face, when the bedroom door creaked open.

Glancing up, she hoped to see Boone. Instead, a concerned Hayley was easing toward her.

"Dallas? Why are you upset? Dad gave you the brooch to make you happy."

The girl's simple statement was enough to help Dallas compose herself and she smiled through her tears.

"Yes. I know that he did. I'm just feeling a little weepy...'cause it's Christmas. And everything is special on Christmas." Sniffing back the last of her tears, she reached out and smoothed an errant strand of hair from Hayley's cheek. "Now, what do you say about you and me going to the kitchen to see what we can find to cook for dinner?"

"Yeah! Can you make mashed potatoes?"

Smiling, Dallas rose to her feet and reached for Hayley's hand. "I think I can manage that."

The two of them exited the room and started down the hallway. "What about macaroni and cheese?" the girl asked.

"If it comes from a box I can."

Hayley giggled. "Oh, Dallas, you're so funny. And I love you."

"I love you, too, sweetie. Very much."

The next day those same words were repeated to Hayley, only this time Dallas's voice was full of tears as the three of them stood out in the bright sunshine and said their final goodbyes. As the snow had melted, her heart had begun to break and when she'd finally driven away from White River Ranch, she'd had to face the fact that Christmas with her Mustang Man was truly over.

Chapter Twelve

Nearly a month later on a cold Friday night, Dallas was sitting in her office at Angel Wings Stables when her grandmother Kate came strolling through the door.

It wasn't unusual for the tall, curvy woman to show up at Dallas's riding stables. Kate was as agile as a person in their fifties, and in spite of her eighty-four years she pretty much did what she wanted to do and went where she wanted to go. But the stables were already closed for the night and no one else was around except Dallas and the horses.

"Grandmother! What are you doing out so late?"

The Donovan matriarch walked over to Dallas's desk and took a seat in front of her granddaughter. "I thought I'd drive over here and see what's been keeping you here night after night. Instead of coming home and having dinner with your family."

Kate was a stickler for the family to gather around the

dinner table. It was her way of keeping tabs on everyone and making sure all was well with her flock.

"I'm sorry," Dallas apologized. "I've had several new children enroll in the program and half of them have rather severe physical handicaps. Lass and I have had to come up with all sorts of ingenious straps and buckles to keep them safely in the saddle."

Kate batted a hand through the air. "I've already heard about all that." She pointed at Dallas's desktop and the papers scattered about. "The kids are gone for tonight. What's keeping you here now?"

Shoving a hand through her hair, Dallas sighed. It was obvious her grandmother had shown up to pry. And maybe it was time for someone to dig into the mire of Dallas's miserable thoughts. She needed help from someone.

"I was going through the mail and found this." She picked up a small envelope and handed it to Kate. "It's from Hayley Barnett. She's—"

"I know who she is," Kate interrupted, "she's that horse trainer's daughter."

"See what she has to say," Dallas urged.

Kate pulled out the single sheet of paper and began to read aloud:

"Dear Dallas,
I hope you are doing okay. I sure am missing you.
The ranch was always quiet but it's awful now that
you're gone.
Dad bought me a Thoroughbred mare. She's
solid brown and very sweet. I call her Angel. Dad
says she was part of my Christmas gift. I like her a
lot. And I wish you were here to ride with me.
I haven't seen Dad smile since you left. I hear

him and Mick arguing all the time. It's awful
around here and I wish you would come back and
make us happy again.
Love, Hayley"

As Kate folded the letter and slipped it back into the envelope, Dallas dabbed at her teary eyes.

"Do you have any idea how that letter makes me feel?" Dallas asked.

Leaning forward, Kate placed the envelope on the desk. "I think I have a good idea. You feel like your heart is ripping apart."

Too choked to speak, Dallas merely nodded and Kate said, "When you first came back from Nevada, I could see that you were a changed woman, Dallas. I've watched you struggling to get back into your regular routine, but it's not the same and you're far from happy."

Sighing, Dallas leaned back in her chair. Her grandmother was so right. She'd never been more miserable in her life. Since the day after Christmas, when she'd said a tearful goodbye to Boone and Hayley, nothing had been the same.

"You know, Grandmother, I always believed that no matter what occurred in my life, the Diamond D would always be my place of solace, would always make me happy. But it isn't making me happy now." With a shake of her head, she rose from her chair and began to move aimlessly around the spacious office. "That sounds awful, doesn't it? I have so much here. You, all of my family. This wonderful riding program that helps so many needy children. I should be satisfied. But I guess I never realized that when you give your heart to a man it stays with him, and I'm not doing very well without it."

Kate frowned at her. "Then why the heck aren't you

doing something about it? Moping around here, hiding in your office every night isn't going to fix anything!"

Feeling more helpless than she'd ever felt in her life, Dallas lifted her arms and let them fall to her sides. "What am I supposed to do? Boone sent me away. He doesn't believe I can be happy on White River Ranch."

"Could you?"

"Oh, Grandmother, when I first arrived there, I thought I'd traveled to the end of the earth. It all seemed like nothing but lonely desert. His closest neighbor is ten miles away. There's no cell phone reception and it takes more than forty minutes just to drive into town. And it's so tiny that Hayley has to ride the bus over to the next town just to go to school. Boone has one ranch hand to help him and he doesn't come in every day. Horse buyers do come to look at the mustangs, but I only saw one while I was there. That business won't pick up until spring. But…I don't know how to explain it—there's a stark beauty about the place and it began to grow on me. Now I miss it almost as much as I do Boone and Hayley." She looked directly at her grandmother. "To answer your question—yes, I could be happy there. But how do I convince Boone? He's already had one bad experience with a woman who couldn't deal with his lifestyle. He's afraid to try again."

"Hmmph. And for a long time after that no-account Allen you were afraid to try again. But you have. And if your Boone cares enough, he'll see that he doesn't have a choice in the matter." Rising from the chair, Kate walked over to her granddaughter and curled a comforting arm around her shoulders. "My advice is to quit wasting time. Pack your bags and get up there. Show him that you mean business."

"But he wants me to take time to think and—"

"Think, hell! He's stalling. You get yourself up there and don't give him a chance to say no."

As she peered into her grandmother's strong face, a glimmer of hope stirred inside Dallas. "Do you really think he'll be glad to see me? He hasn't contacted me since I left."

"Have you tried to contact him?"

Dallas shook her head. "No. I thought— I didn't want to push myself on him. I've been waiting—hoping he might call."

"Waiting and hoping might be a good tactic for fishing, but not for catching a man." With a hand at her back, she urged Dallas out of the office. "Come on, honey. Let's go home and I'll help you pack."

Where the hell was she? Boone raced through the barn, desperately hoping he'd find Hayley tucked away in some dark corner, but there was no sight of her. And with Angel in her stall, and Rock out in the corral, he knew his daughter wasn't out riding. He'd already hunted through the house and there'd been no Hayley there, either.

As soon as he'd picked her up at the school bus stop this evening, he'd driven straight home and let her out at the house. After that, Boone had saddled up and ridden out to work on one of the windmill pumps. When he'd returned a half hour ago, she'd been gone and now he could only fear the worst.

Had she run away? Had some evil person come to the ranch and hauled her away? Oh, God, it was getting dark and he had to do something!

Racing back to the house, he realized he had no other choice but to call the sheriff's department. They might not consider her a missing child, but Boone sure as hell did. She was a responsible girl. She didn't just go off on her own without consulting him first!

Inside the kitchen, he was about to reach for the phone, when it suddenly rang. He jerked up the receiver and then practically cursed out loud when he heard his father's voice on the other end.

"Dad, I don't have time to talk now. Hayley is missing and—"

"Hayley isn't missing. She's with me."

Totally stunned, Boone stared blindly at the wall in front of him. "What? Where?"

"At my house in town. I picked her up at the ranch a couple of hours ago."

"You—why?"

"She called me. Asked me if I'd come get her. I told her I would. I could tell she was unhappy and I thought it would be better than her trying to run away."

Thank God his daughter was safe and that his father sounded perfectly sober. But there were a wad of questions rolling through Boone's head, far too many to be hashed out over the phone.

"I'll be there shortly."

"Boone, I wouldn't be too hard on her. She's pretty upset."

Since when had Newt cared about his granddaughter's emotional health? Boone wondered grimly.

You've not exactly shown a wealth of understanding to your daughter lately, Boone. For the past month, ever since Dallas left, you've known that Hayley was depressed and moody. But you haven't done anything to make things better for her.

How could he? He didn't even know how to help himself, much less help his daughter to get past the pain of losing Dallas. Hayley blamed him for letting Dallas go, for not asking her to marry him and become a part of the family.

And now Boone could only blame himself for this whole mess.

When he arrived at Newt's house in Pioche, his father and Hayley were sitting at the kitchen table playing checkers. She shot Boone a cold, stony look, but Newt was more affable and invited his son to take a seat.

Hayley turned an accusing glare on her grandfather. "You told him I was here!"

"I had to, honey. He would have been worried sick about you."

"No. He wouldn't have!" she practically shouted. "He doesn't care about anyone but himself!"

Before either man could stop her, the girl jumped to her feet and ran from the room. Boone started to go after her, but Newt quickly caught him by the arm.

"Let her go for right now."

Boone couldn't ever remember a time that Newt had given him orders. Maybe if he had, if he'd shown enough interest to give his son orders, then things would have been different for the two of them.

Easing down in the chair across from his father, Boone let out a long, weary breath. "I understand she's been unhappy with me lately. But what in the world set her off like this today? She was okay when I picked her up at the bus stop."

Newt rose to his feet and shuffled over to the cabinet, where he began to put a fresh pot of coffee on to brew. It was a damned sight better than seeing him splash whiskey into a shot glass. "One of her best friends didn't show up for school today because her mother had just had a baby—a boy. Hayley is jealous of her, you know. She wants brothers and sisters, too. She wants to be like her friends."

"Hell, Dad, I don't even have a wife. How does she expect me to give her siblings? She's too young to understand—"

"She's almost a teenager. She understands much more than you think," Newt interrupted. "From what I can gather, she's pretty cut up about this Dallas from New Mexico. Hayley had somehow gotten her hopes up that you were gonna marry this woman."

Boone helplessly shook his head. "I want to." Just admitting it made him feel better, but it sure didn't fix anything. "But it's not that simple."

"Why not? She doesn't love you?"

Boone grimaced. "She says she loves me."

Newt walked back over to the table. "So what's the deal?"

Boone's shoulders slumped with defeat. "The ranch. She'd never be happy there. You know what it's like. I could never ask another woman to live there. It wouldn't be fair or right."

Newt opened his mouth to speak and Boone braced himself for another long pitch to sell the place. But that didn't happen. Instead, his father sank back into a chair and studied his son for long, thoughtful moments.

"Boone, I'm gonna tell you something. Something that I should've told you a long time ago. I just wasn't man enough to do it."

"Dad—"

He held up a hand to halt Boone's protest. "Don't worry, I'm not going to start lecturing you about selling the place. That—well, since your mother died I've been thinking a lot about things. Guess that's about all I have to do anymore is to think. Anyway, I was wrong to push you to sell. But that's not the issue now. You're letting White River Ranch ruin your life. Just like I did. And that's a waste. A shameful waste."

Boone stared at him as he tried to comprehend. "You blame the ranch for your problems? That's—"

"Hell, no! I made my own problems. That's what I'm trying to say. All these years I've felt sorry for myself. I blamed the ranch for everything."

"Because you didn't like it? Because you never wanted to leave Arizona? That's hardly any reason to feel sorry for yourself."

The older man's gaze dropped to the tabletop and for the first time that Boone could ever remember, he saw real sincerity on his father's face.

"There was more to it than that, Boone. I let hatred fill me, consume me until...well, hardly anything else mattered. You see, there was more to it than what you were ever told. When I was in junior high, I made the decision that I wanted to be a doctor. I worked very hard to make perfect grades in all the right subjects. I wanted everything to go in my favor so that I would be accepted to a good medical school. Your grandparents went along with my plans and saved money for my college education. I contributed to the fund by working through the summers mowing lawns and sacking groceries at a local supermarket. I didn't expect them to pay everything for me. I was more than willing to work to reach my goal."

A doctor? His father had wanted to be a doctor! It was a stunning revelation. One that Boone could hardly wrap his thoughts around. And yet, he could see for himself that the old man wasn't lying. "So what happened?"

"By the time I reached my senior year in high school your granddad decided he was tired of mining. He wanted a ranch and when he saw White River he wouldn't let anything stop him from getting it. He used all of my college funds to buy the place. I was—" He shook his head. "I was devastated and so angry I couldn't see straight. He'd squashed my dreams to find his. After that, I decided nothing mattered. I decided if my parents hadn't cared any more for me than that, then to hell with them."

Boone felt as if he'd been kicked in the gut. All these years he'd never understood Newt's behavior. He'd thought of him as a worthless rebel, when all along he'd actually been a crushed young man. "Why didn't you tell me this before, Dad?"

Newt looked at him bleakly. "You thought the sun rose and fell on your grandparents. And I'd never been much good for you anyway. I didn't want to make things worse by trying to paint them in a bad light."

"So why did you decide to tell me tonight?"

"Hayley. I don't want to see that damned ranch wreck her life, too. I don't want to see you obsess over a piece of land when you could have the love of a good woman, the devotion of a wonderful daughter. You got to give a little, Boone, or you're going to live the rest of your life alone."

Boone wiped a hand over his face, then slowly rose to his feet. "I'd better go talk with her."

"Boone?"

He looked down at his dad and was surprised to see a faint smile on the man's face. "Ever since Christmas I've been trying my best not to drink. And this evening when Hayley called me—I was glad. Just to have her ask me for help did something to me in here." He tapped his chest. "I've made some awful mistakes in my life. Instead of letting myself get all festered with hate, I should've been working to be what I wanted to be. I missed the boat with you, son. But from now on I can at least try to be a good grandfather to Hayley."

His throat tight with emotions, Boone patted his father's shoulder. "I've made mistakes, too, Dad. But from now on I promise things are going to be different. For all of us."

Two days later, Boone and Hayley shoved the last of their suitcases into the backseat of the truck. It was Monday and normally Hayley would be in school, but Boone had talked with her teachers about letting her catch up on the classes she would be missing while they were gone for a week to New Mexico.

As Boone shut the truck door and mentally went over a checklist in his head, Hayley asked, "Will Mick make sure that Miss Holiday and her babies get fed?"

"The cat food is in the barn. He's promised to take care of them. Along with Angel and Queenie and everybody else around here with a mouth," Boone assured his daughter.

Hayley smiled, but just as quickly another worried look returned to her face. "But what if Dallas isn't home? She might be gone with her brother to the racetrack or something. Then what will we do? Go find her? I think you should call first, Dad. Wouldn't that be the smart thing to do?"

If he had to, Boone would go to the ends of the earth to find Dallas. But whether she would be glad to see him was another matter. When he'd first decided to drive down to New Mexico and propose to her, he'd wanted to do it as a surprise. And he sure didn't want to give Dallas the chance to turn him down over the phone. But Hayley's concerns were making him have second thoughts. Maybe he should call and make sure she'd be there? After all, a thousand miles wasn't just a little leisurely drive.

"Okay. Let's go back in the house and I'll call before we leave."

Taking his daughter by the shoulder, he urged her back toward the yard gate, but halfway there, she suddenly pointed to something in the distance. "Look, Dad. Someone is coming. Reckon it's a horse buyer? You won't let them stay long, will you?"

Boone squinted at the red pickup truck barreling up the driveway toward the ranch house. "I don't have a buyer coming that I know of. But don't worry, I'll tell him or her that we have plans and need to leave."

The truck braked to a quick stop and he stared in disbelief as he read the insignia on the door. Angel Wings Stables Diamond D Ranch.

"Dad! It's Dallas! It's Dallas!" Hayley yelled as she began running toward the vehicle.

Boone's heart swelled as he hurried to embrace the only woman he would ever love.

Epilogue

More than a year later on White River Ranch, Dallas wrapped her three-month-old son in a heavy blanket and carried him across the hard-packed ranch yard until she reached the big barn. Behind it, in a round training pen, Boone and Mick had been showing horses for the most of the afternoon. Now the last buyer was about to leave and Dallas waited in a secluded spot from the wind while Boone shook the man's hand.

Once the buyer had driven away, Boone walked over to his wife and son.

"You must have sold something," Dallas said with a grin. "You're smiling."

"I'm smiling because I didn't sell her. He wanted Fancy and I told him I couldn't let her go. She was going to belong to our son one day." He smacked a kiss on her cheek and then on the top of his son's red hair. "So what are you and little Bodie doing out in the cold? Were you missing me that much?" he teased.

"It's not that cold," Dallas insisted. "The sun is bright and warm today. It's almost like spring is around the corner."

"The sight of you two is just like spring to me," he said with a grin.

Smiling, Dallas repaid him for the compliment with a kiss on his cheek. "Actually, I walked down here to see Mick," she said slyly. "But I don't see him around."

Boone howled. "Mick! He's got enough female attention without getting it from mine."

Dallas laughed. "I only wanted to invite him to dinner this evening. I'm having your dad over, too. As a celebration of sorts for Hayley winning a spot in the choir trio at school."

"That's nice of you, honey. I'm sure Mick will want to stay and eat. I'll ask him later. Now that all the buyers are gone, he's ridden out to the west pasture to check on the calves."

"Oh. So we're alone," she said, her eyes twinkling suggestively.

This time Boone laughed as he lifted Bodie from his mother's arms and snuggled his son close to his chest. "Not quite. Bodie is here to make sure his parents don't get too frisky."

As Dallas watched her husband carry their son over to the dusty horse pen, she could only think how much her life had changed since she'd first come to White River Ranch so many months ago.

She and Boone had been married in a simple, but beautiful ceremony in the church at Pioche where Father O'Quinn had declared them man and wife. Later, in order to include her family, they had celebrated with a huge reception on the Diamond D. And since that time, the sharing between families and ranches was still continuing.

In winter, while Hayley attended school, they remained on White River and Boone stayed busy training his mustangs. In summer they traveled down to the Diamond D and spent those months in the cool mountain climate with her family, while Mick kept the ranch going here.

At first, she'd been shocked that Boone had even suggested living away from White River for any amount of time. And she'd been afraid that he would be bored and miserable once he was away from it. But to her surprise and delight, he'd settled right in and now he was looking forward to helping her brothers build a string of quarter horses to begin racing at Ruidoso Downs. As for Hayley, the girl was over the moon at having a new little brother and she was counting the days until they returned to the Diamond D, where she was more than happy to help out at Angel Wings Stables.

Joining her husband and son, Dallas gazed out at the milling horses. Fancy had foaled not more than two weeks ago and already her sorrel colt was bucking and running with strong, sturdy legs.

"That one will be just about right for Bodie," Dallas said with a little laugh. "I have a feeling our son is going to want to get in the saddle before he can ever walk."

Boone slipped a loving arm around the back of her waist. "But if he doesn't want to be a cowboy, that will be all right, too," he murmured thoughtfully.

She glanced up at him. "You're thinking about your dad now."

His mood suddenly pensive, Boone nodded. "Every person has dreams, Dallas. And sometimes a child's dreams are far different than those of his parents. I'd always said I never wanted to be like my father, but damned if I wasn't slowly making the same mistakes he'd made. I was thinking of myself and my wants more than Hayley's. I thank God you came along and opened my eyes to so many things."

In the past year, Newt had been working to make himself into a better person. He'd determinedly weaned himself off alcohol and was now doing volunteer work at a hospital over in Caliente. Slowly, he and Boone were building a relationship and seeing them together made Dallas very happy. "Your father is doing quite well now. Once he realized that Hayley needed him, it changed his whole outlook."

He looked down at her. "Yeah. All of us want to be needed," he said gently. "And I need you and our children more than anything in my life."

Rising up on her toes, she planted a swift kiss on his mouth, then reached for Bodie. "Well, you're going to need a cook if I don't get back to the house and get dinner started."

She turned to go, then paused, prompting Boone to ask teasingly, "What's the matter? Decide you'd rather kiss than cook?"

She pulled a playful face at him. "It's a pleasant thought. But actually, I just remembered to tell you that I spoke with my brother Conall this morning. He says that Liam is shipping a bunch of runners out to California and plans to stay there with them through the Hollywood spring meet."

Boone's brows lifted. "Is that unusual for him? You sound puzzled."

Dallas shrugged. "Well, he always ships runners to California at this time of the year. But he never stays that long. Something isn't clicking with him as usual."

"Hmm. I'm sure it has something to do with the purses

or the racing schedule. Or it could be he simply wants to stay out there and enjoy the warmer climate."

Dallas rolled her eyes. "Are you kidding? The only time Liam notices the climate is when he's studying the condition of the track. No. There's something else behind this. And I'm just wondering if he's found a woman."

"A woman?" Boone repeated with a flicker of interest.

"That's what I'm hoping. Liam needs to learn there's more to life than crisscrossing back and forth across the United States racing horses."

Chuckling softly, Boone pulled her and their son into the warm circle of his arms. "What Liam needs to learn about is sharing. That's what love is all about."

As Dallas's lips met her husband's, she murmured, "Mmm. Sharing. You couldn't have spoken a nicer word, my darling."

* * * * *

HEART & HOME

Heartwarming romances where love can
happen right when you least expect it.

◆ Harlequin®
SPECIAL EDITION®

COMING NEXT MONTH
AVAILABLE DECEMBER 27, 2011

#2161 FORTUNE'S CINDERELLA
The Fortunes of Texas: Whirlwind Romance
Karen Templeton

#2162 MOMMY IN THE MAKING
Northbridge Nuptials
Victoria Pade

#2163 DOCTORS IN THE WEDDING
Doctors in the Family
Gina Wilkins

#2164 THE DADDY DANCE
Mindy Klasky

#2165 THE HUSBAND RECIPE
Linda Winstead Jones

#2166 MADE FOR MARRIAGE
Helen Lacey

SPECIAL EDITION

Life, Love and Family

Karen Templeton

introduces

The FORTUNES *of* TEXAS: Whirlwind Romance

When a tornado destroys Red Rock, Texas, Christina Hastings finds herself trapped in the rubble with telecommunications heir Scott Fortune. He's handsome, smart and everything Christina has learned to guard herself against. As they await rescue, an unlikely attraction forms between the two and Scott soon finds himself wanting to know about this mysterious beauty. But can he catch Christina before she runs away from her true feelings?

FORTUNE'S CINDERELLA

Available December 27th wherever books are sold!

*Brittany Grayson survived a horrible ordeal at the hands
of a serial killer known as The Professional…
who's after her now?*

*Harlequin® Romantic Suspense presents a new installment
in Carla Cassidy's reader-favorite miniseries,*
LAWMEN OF BLACK ROCK.

Enjoy a sneak peek of
TOOL BELT DEFENDER.

*Available January 2012
from Harlequin® Romantic Suspense.*

"**B**rittany?" His voice was deep and pleasant and made
her realize she'd been staring at him openmouthed through
the screen door.

"Yes, I'm Brittany and you must be…" Her mind suddenly went blank.

"Alex. Alex Crawford, Chad's friend. You called him
about a deck?"

As she unlocked the screen, she realized she wasn't
quite ready yet to allow a stranger inside, especially a male
stranger.

"Yes, I did. It's nice to meet you, Alex. Let's walk around
back and I'll show you what I have in mind," she said. She
frowned as she realized there was no car in her driveway.
"Did you walk here?" she asked.

His eyes were a warm blue that stood out against his
tanned face and was complemented by his slightly shaggy
dark hair. "I live three doors up." He pointed up the street to
the Walker home that had been on the market for a while.

"How long have you lived there?"

"I moved in about six weeks ago," he replied as they

walked around the side of the house.

That explained why she didn't know the Walkers had moved out and Mr. Hard Body had moved in. Six weeks ago she'd still been living at her brother Benjamin's house trying to heal from the trauma she'd lived through.

As they reached the backyard she motioned toward the broken brick patio just outside the back door. "What I'd like is a wooden deck big enough to hold a barbecue pit and an umbrella table and, of course, lots of people."

He nodded and pulled a tape measure from his tool belt. "An outdoor entertainment area," he said.

"Exactly," she replied and watched as he began to walk the site. The last thing Brittany had wanted to think about over the past eight months of her life was men. But looking at Alex Crawford definitely gave her a slight flutter of pure feminine pleasure.

Will Brittany be able to heal in the arms of Alex, her hotter-than-sin handyman...or will a second psychopath silence her forever? Find out in
TOOL BELT DEFENDER
Available January 2012
from Harlequin® Romantic Suspense
wherever books are sold.